THE CARTELS' ERROR

Book Four of the Cody Hunter Series

Hallen Taylor

Author's Tranquility Press
Marietta, Georgia

Hallen Taylor /Author's Tranquility Press
2706 Station Club Drive SW
Marietta, GA 30060
www.authorstranquilitypress.com

Publisher's Note: This is a work of fiction. Names, characters, places, and incidents are a product of the author's imagination. Locales and public names are sometimes used for atmospheric purposes. Any resemblance to actual people, living or dead, or to businesses, companies, events, institutions, or locales is completely coincidental.

Ordering Information:
Quantity sales. Special discounts are available on quantity purchases by corporations, associations, and others. For details, contact the "Special Sales Department" at the address above.

The Cartels Error: Book Four of the Cody Hunter Series /Hallen Taylor
Paperback   ISBN: 978-1-957208-14-5
eBook   ISBN: 978-1-957208-15-2

For
My best friend
Wanda Hunter Taylor

Forward

This concludes the epic Cody Hunter series of four.

Due to his exceptional talent with firearms and his ability to move fast, Cody was drafted into an elite, highly secretive organization of only a few men with the same gifts.

Cody paired with two men that could move and shoot like comic book heroes. They explained the ropes to him on the job while he endured their own brand of humor and harmless initiation processes that never ceased.

The three of them first played with two highly successful cartels headquartered between Bogota, Medellin. Next, they flew to Iraq to crush Saddam Hussein's prodigious accumulation of nuclear weapons. As soon as they concluded their stay in Iraq, they unknowingly assisted President Reagan's Star Wars Project in Hawaii.

After almost three years, the cartels hid a small band of expensive mercenaries to seek out and destroy the trio in the United States. This was their error.

CHAPTER 1

TUCSON, ARIZONA. 1984

Cody Hunter stood quietly, strangely disconcerted with the telephone in his hand. Having not heard from his chief in weeks, perhaps months, then suddenly he received an unexpected call. All this time elapsed. He thought his job had dwindled into oblivion, and rightfully so.

His mind raced through several facts he already hoped to forget. Everyone warned him to not marry while working this job.

His hand trembled slightly, and he, a young man of thirty-three, had considered himself imperturbable, an athletic man at six-one without loose flesh over his well-toned body, began to shake. He stood helplessly in the calm setting of the living room of his Tucson home. His right hand held the telephone too tight, and all the man said, "Good morning. How are you?"

He loved his new life with a new bride who had a tiny son when they met. The same little guy busied himself playing at his feet.

He attempted to draw a breath and return the greeting. He liked his employer, whom he called Dan, the station chief in the Bogota Station in Colombia.

A second hardly expired from Dan's friendly greeting before Cody began thinking many thoughts again. He voiced a few words. "I'm retired, Dan. You okayed it and even blessed my decision."

"Now, hold on a second, Cody." Dan said calmly. "If this wasn't urgent I would have allowed you to be forgotten-- permanently. Actually, you never officially retired. You don't even know where we've kept all your wages, which is a tidy sum by now. I guess you have forgotten about the money you have coming."

Cody felt nerves attacking his entire body. Fear overwhelmed him, not for himself but for his family. He literally dreaded to displease his wife as well as his boss. He owed Dan, who drafted him into the work long before Cody knew anything about it or even aware that anything like such a well-paying job existed. Nevertheless, he wanted to stop his chief before he said another word.

"Dan, my toddler step-son is playing on my feet as we're talking. Nothing can move me out of this room. As much as I respect you as a man and as a supervisor, I am settled down and nothing is going to change that."

"Cody, do you remember those two cartel headquarters that you and your buddies shot up? You burned most of the buildings to the ground. My point is, they haven't forgotten. So—at this time—they have a fresh lead on you through Bob.

"Now listen up! They hired U. S. born mercenaries to even the score. Yes, they want all three of you dead! Now, that will include your families and all your loved ones. Dead! You guys left their billion dollar businesses in ashes. They are all out for revenge! Here's the bad part of the news, I fear they may have already caught Bob."

"How could they know this, Dan? We were one of the most secretive forces in the world. And no one is slyer, faster or tougher than Bob. What makes you think they could have taken him?"

"Because he disappeared while I was in the act of telling him about the cartels hiring these killers! This was less than an hour ago, Cody. Bob planned retirement but he had not claimed his wages. My source is my old general buddy in Bogota, who now resides in the capital building of Colombia as president of this great southern nation. We still talk. He uses me and my men regularly and actually wants his country drug free. Somebody in his office sold you guys out. So make your wife and kid safe right now and call me back. If not, listen up again! I'll be brief."

Cody's small son, trying to talk, slapped at his shiny boots with a rag toy. He loved Cody's full time attention. Presently, the time arrived for him to swipe and pound feet and legs. Cody paused and watched him, smiling hopelessly, not wanting to hear anything more from Dan.

"Dan," Cody uttered weakly, "Did your source mention Tucson or where Bob lives in Tennessee?"

"No. He mentioned Bob's brother's hangout in Memphis. I have an idea they started there."

"No one knows my home or present name. We'll stay."

"Fine, Cody. But I want you to go bail Leo out of jail in Israel. They know he's there. You are all that I have left out of this detail. Leo called me yesterday and wants out of jail without delay. I think he still believes his bride is alive somewhere over there. I want you to take him to help you find Bob. Make it today if not sooner! I want you guys to teach those hired mercenaries better manners. After that, feel free to cause those two cartels to die and burn again."

Cody began to think. Dan came across sincerely. He ran a secret organization that often kept their country free in a world dominated by powerful dictators. Dan understood his three men, all he possessed in the elite force he operated. He only acted as a D.E.A. Station Chief in Bogota, yet dictators like Saddam Hussein and dangerous heads of countries across the world only existed because this man had not received word from the president to put an end to their evil.

Dan sighed and apologized. "We don't have the recruits to replace you three guys, Cody. You, yourself, were our last real recruit. I admit to thinking we thought that our outfit was retired, also. It isn't! You three men are in a pot full of serious trouble. Believe me, old son, I have the highest respect for your family."

Cody swallowed hard. "Our little organization appeared practically cancelled, anyway, Dan. I know we failed miserably in Iraq, but that can still be fixed. The three of us stopped working Iraq after absorbing all those bullets, but we're alive now and good as new."

Dan raised his voice only slightly. "Cody, listen to me! Our organization will last until you three men are retired or erased from this earth. I know that you and Leo are alive but Bob has disappeared and he did it while I was talking with him!"

Cody held the receiver tightly to his ear and leaned over to gently caress the happy little face of his son. "I'm listening, Dan. The good Lord knows that I will do what's necessary to protect my family."

"Okay, first, you guys will not return to Iraq to finish that job! Get that out of your heads! Heaven knows it needs to happen but the president believes that his military will bring that monster to his knees."

"That's not going to happen, Dan, and you know it. Saddam lives for the world's attention. He's slowly wiping Kurdistan off the face of the globe and he practically has the whole world supporting him on account of the oil that was found under Kurdistan soil."

"Cody, listen up! Forget Iraq! I only have a minute or two left on this secure line. Bob is out of reach at this very crucial time. I had no sooner told him of the mercenaries when he dropped the telephone. There's not a trace of him, Cody! He was living peacefully in the woods of his beloved Tennessee. We were talking each week or so. When I broke the news to him less than an hour ago, he didn't even bother to hang up. He left the phone dangling. That is not Bob! Find him!"

"He always hangs up on you, Dan. Maybe he just missed the cradle."

"Cody, you're not listening! Unlike you and Leo, you can bet Bob would always hang up on me when he was through talking.

This time he wasn't through talking. I'm scared they caught him at the telephone!"

"Okay, now it's time for you to listen up, Dan. Strangers don't sneak up on Bob. It simply doesn't happen and it will never happen. If he's dead they shot him from a distance. You would've heard the bullet strike him. Bob is fast and dangerous up close, so they do not have him. Period! He is going after the love of his life. That's all. Stop your worrying! Better yet: Why don't you ever worry about me and Leo?"

"Well said, Cody. Excellent question! **Now**--get yourself over to Jerusalem before I really give *you* something to worry about!"

"Okay, but as of this morning, I'm back on the payroll. I still have all my credit cards."

Dan scoffed. "You're already overpaid! I'm kidding. You're going to be paid! Now zip it and let me finish!"

Cody almost grinned. "I'm busy so talk fast!" He looked about the room for his wife, Nancy, who worked silently and alone in her office in the next room. Charley, his toddler, jabbered happy noises as he slapped his wet hands on Cody's glossy--shined boots.

"Now—Cody, concerning Leo, he didn't sound exactly like himself to me. Take it slow with him and find out if all of his stars are still positioned correctly in the galaxy. You with me thus far?"

"Dan, the last I heard from Leo was that he wasn't leaving Israel. His Israeli bride is there and he's not leaving."

Dan cut him off. "I heard from Leo yesterday! I held off calling you until today. Leo is in prison, Cody! He's locked up in a stinking Israeli jail! They have refused to allow him to call for weeks, maybe months! But, as of his telephone call, I think that they're ready to cut him loose."

Cody spoke calmly. "So why haven't they?"

"Because he keeps knocking guards unconscious! That gets his sentence compounded each time. They've forced tranquilizers down him until the doctor has refused to give him more. They're tired of spending good money on his medication, so they have decided to shoot him with real bullets or else turn him over to American authorities. Those were his exact words."

Cody looked down at Charley, who now sat uncomfortably on both of his boots. "Well, boss, you already know that Leo has a flair for comedy. But...since Christmas is rapidly falling on us as we speak, anything else on the mercenaries, how many or where?"

"Nothing, get out of town and let them find you. But go to Israel and make Leo safe first and foremost. Seriously, watch Leo closely. He may be broken after weeks in a jail."

"Okay, boss. I can leave within the hour, as usual, but I think my control over him is rather limited when comparing it with yours and Bob's."

"Oh—by the way, Cody, since I have your attention, the mercenaries are paid big bucks to torture all three of you to death under a doctor's close scrutiny. The entire process will be filmed, which includes all the sound effects. In other words, they're planning on making you three guys suffer as many days as possible."

"Stop enjoying yourself, Dan."

"I can't tell you much more. You are hereby advised that all three of you are still on your own. No one but me, Red, and the press in our entire government know that you exist. Even your wages that we banked for you were all stolen from the CIA, NSA and the FBI's budgets. If the FBI ever finds out about it, you're going to have a brand new set of enemies. The cartels have given the mercenaries unlimited expense accounts and all of the latest technology to try and find you. My advice for you is to find Bob alive. From there the three of you will survive by on the job training."

Cody said, "Dan, how do you know your phone isn't bugged?"

"You let me worry about that! Now, listen up, this job may take you weeks. But after you deal with them, get over to Bogota and do another number on those cartels. You'll have the president's backing, except for manpower and money, of course."

Cody hesitated before speaking. "You know that Leo believes that his wife is still alive, don't you?"

"Yes. You've got to help him get over that, too. It doesn't matter if she faked her death or not. Israel needs her. She needs to help get her country back in shape. Leo cannot help her."

Cody lifted his son up to his height and hugged him. "Leo loves her. He might as well remain in prison."

"Okay," Dan replied. "Whatever! But I'm counting on you, Cody, to get him *out* of prison."

"Big mistake," Cody replied.

Dan grinned over the telephone. "Now don't go over there planning to bust him out of jail or anything like that. Be nice. The Israelis want to turn him loose. Then, handle Leo with kid gloves until you know that he's his old self."

"Okay, boss. I'll fly over there, pay his fines, and pick his brain while I accompany him to where we find Bob. If Leo is kosher, we'll find Bob."

"Good boy! You sound almost as reliable as Bob. I'm serious now, Cody. Please know that I'll be glad to do what I can to support you, which will be absolutely nothing! *Zilch!* But my heart's in the right place, Cody. I just want you to know that!"

Cody grinned at Dan's poor stab at humor. "You've worked for the Justice Department too long to ever be a politician, Dan."

Cody then slammed the receiver back in its cradle without another word. He cuddled his son before snatching his ready-packed bag from the shelf. He walked into Nancy's office. Her eyes had already collected tears. Cody's heart felt as if it might stop at any second.

"You're leaving, aren't you?"

"This is bad, dear. I won't lie to you. The Colombians are retaliating here in our back yard. I'm leaving in order to deal with them out of earshot. They are out for revenge. Just hang in where you are, dear. You'll be okay. Don't try to contact me. I'll try and call when I can. It may be days."

"Cody, I don't like this. I'm scared! Charley is only a baby. What if they come here?"

"They won't. They don't have the leads."

"I want you here with us!"

"So, do I. But we have to play it as if they don't have a clue. Bob, Leo and I can fight them in many states away where you won't be involved."

"Don't leave us, Cody. We need you!"

Cody fought back tears. He failed to control his voice. "It has to be our way, sweetheart. Just remember that I love you both more than I love my own life. I cannot put it any other way. Keep your faith and wait for me. If the unthinkable happens, please tell Charley when he's old enough that I loved him."

CHAPTER 2

Cody's name never existed anywhere on government files, so he didn't stop by the U. S. Consulate after arriving in Israel. His taxi carried him straight to the Army base's nearest gate. The officer on duty proved friendly and called for a car once he learned the purpose of the visit. They drove straight to the military prison that suffered the most unpopular Irishman in Israel.

Preliminary paperwork and a thorough body search didn't take long. He walked the corridors with male and female guards. He noticed many somber Arabs in cells as he passed. He spotted one American who watched him pass with a hungry stare. Cody hardly recognized Leo the Lion without a shave and haircut in months. The five guards, armed with spray and Tasers, cautiously opened the iron door at Cody's nod.

He stepped inside and reached for Leo's loose shirt covering his broad shoulders. Without a word, the two men hugged in a brotherly greeting. After a brief moment of back patting, Leo spoke as he fought against tears.

"It took you long enough to get here, home boy. Where's Bob?"

Cody kept his eyes locked on Leo's for any type of peculiarity that didn't belong. "Bob has disappeared somewhere in

Memphis. I'm guessing he's near the coal mines in West Virginia where his little sweetie lives. This was yesterday. I'll explain later. For now, be content to know that all three of us are in major trouble! Our lives will be worthless once we step back on U.S. soil. Bob and I need you in one piece, so let's get 10-8 without you making anymore enemies over here."

Leo threw both hands into the air and exclaimed, "It's about time! This vacation is a long way from the Bahamas. Let's go back and finish our job in Iraq!"

Cody didn't move. "Is your business here over or just put aside?"

"These pukes that are now looking at us have put my wife undercover and keep showing me papers of her death. That's all bull! They know where she is!"

"Leo, what they have is the best information that you're ever going to get. If she's alive, and if she wants you, you will know it. If she's dead, then you're going to spend the rest of your life without her. That's the best I can offer you. Let's give her another year or so to reappear. Okay?"

Leo looked at the guards. "Why couldn't they just say that instead of poking those phony papers under my nose all the time?"

Cody gritted his teeth against Leo's refusal to cut the guards a little slack. "Look, they aren't lying to you! They all insisted that she was dead because that's what they're ordered to say! Let 'em alone!"

"Well, their stupidity and a lack of respect earned them a few busted lips!"

Cody never touched him and turned to leave. Leo followed close behind. Once he came even with Cody, he turned to the guards. "Find my clothes, all of them, and my money! This man will let me starve if I don't have money. I'm almost starved, anyway! Your food is poor in comparison with good Arab food! Speaking of which, there's no telling how many Arabs I've eaten in this British type dungeon."

The man who released Leo shoved his clothes at him and counted the money before releasing it. Leo counted it after the man counted it, even though he knew better. Cody felt the air grow tenser and wished Leo would lighten just a bit.

When no one said anything, Leo could keep quiet no longer. "I don't like this place because it stinks like Arab urine and dirty underwear. Did you know there is a big shortage of soap here?"

The red-faced clerk pointed to a door. "Change your clothes in there!"

Leo dropped his pants and shucked his shirt where he stood. "You change in there! I want real clothes on my body right now!"

Two female guards stopped and watched, not for curiosity but for assistance in the event the guards decided to teach Leo additional manners.

Leo left his prison clothes on the floor and nodded to Cody, "Let's go unless you want to stay and visit with God's chosen people."

The commercial flight to New York City had its share of lay overs but they skipped Leo's home town of Boston. They used one stop for shaves and haircuts. Leo began to breathe and move with the bounce Cody used to see in him. He found flowers for his mother in an airport gift shop and sent them to her under an assumed name.

"With these," he explained, "she knows I'm still alive and love her very much. She also expects to spend a few days with me in the Bahamas. But her poor soul has to shamefully wait until we find Bob's wine-soaked body and hang him out to dry for a week or two."

Cody nodded, not really caring to hear about Leo's non-existent plans for the Bahamas. He said, "Leo, speaking of time, I don't like being away from my little son. He likes to sit on my feet and chew his fingers while he's cutting his first teeth."

Leo grinned. "As soon as my lady comes out of hiding, we're going to have one of those playing at my feet. We'll call him Cody Bob or Bob Cody. I don't know which."

Cody said, "You will call him whatever your wife wishes to call him, which will be David, perhaps, Moses, or Jeremiah."

They stopped in the city of Memphis where they looked up the only family member Bob ever mentioned, an older brother. This brother scraped out a meager living betting on pool players at his favorite parlor. They worked through the smoke and noisy tables before finding him silently occupying a seat next to the wall. He looked up and announced his only explanation of where Bob might be.

"You know, I would think that you guys would know where Dennis might be by now. It ain't been a week since a few of you were trying to look him up."

"Who looked him up?" Leo asked. "It wasn't any of our company."

The brother of Bob appeared exasperated. "You guys! Whoever the hell you are, C.I.A. or some sort of feds that don't like answering questions but they sure as hell like asking 'em!"

"Did you see any identification on them?" Leo asked.

"I don't remember seeing anything! They bought me a pint of Hooligan's Row and a pack of cigarettes. That's more than what you guys have offered."

Leo looked inside his wallet and presented him a twenty-dollar bill. "Listen, brother, we may be the only friends that Dennis has in this whole world. We know him as Bob. His life may be in danger as we speak, if he isn't already dead. None of our people has bothered to look him up! Nobody! Those were the bad guys that you saw looking for him. Bob was here on vacation and no one knew where he was, except us. We only knew he was in Memphis. Tell us what you can about those imposters."

"Well, I told them that he used to have a lady friend whose dad worked the coal mines in West Virginia. They left on that information."

"What did they look like? Were they well-dressed or black or white or what?"

Bob's brother looked at the twenty. "Do you have any more of these things? I'm going through some bad times, you know."

Leo presented him another twenty. "We like Bob, your brother! We want to find him alive. I would think that you would, too."

He snatched the money and said, "I wouldn't worry none about Dennis if I was you. He can take care of himself. Have you guys ever seen him fight? I have. Dennis is fast, man! I made a bundle off him one time when they matched him up in a street fight. Man--that fight didn't last a second!

"The funny part was that Dennis was the underdog. Ha! I collected some bills off that one! I knew Dennis, you see. They didn't. They gave me two to one odds. Ha!"

Both Cody and Leo stood up and patted Bob's brother on his shoulder. They understood, sadly, why Bob seldom visited home. On their way out, they walked hurt due to having no new leads to Bob's whereabouts.

The bartender had watched them and Bob's brother the whole time they talked and even heard part of the conversation. He walked from behind the bar and hailed them.

"Wait up, guys! Come on over and I'll pour you a drink. Leo smiled and met the man half-way. Thank you, sir! We were looking for a friend. I don't suppose you know him. He's that man's brother, Dennis."

The bartender introduced himself to both men. "I overheard why you were here. Let me tell you something, the older brother, there, is always bragging about Dennis being somebody big in the C.I.A. or F.B.I. or something. He's done it for years. He scratches out a living by saying anything that he thinks will be interesting enough to earn him money."

Cody said, "We know him as Bob. We or he aren't C.I.A. or anything of the sort. We aren't anybody. How do you know Dennis?"

"High school buddies. What Mack said about Dennis is true. He was a star running back on our football team and took us to state each year he played. He made a lot of friends. His parents and sister died in an automobile crash. I dated the sister. We would've been married and had a bunch of kids by now."

"Sorry to hear that," Leo said. "Do you remember the men that Dennis's brother mentioned?"

The bartender nodded affirmatively. "Oh boy, do I! Mack wasn't interested in anything but what they offered him. It burned me up. Dennis came by and said hello way last April. He was on vacation. "

They listened, "Who do you think those men were?"

The bartender said, "Gangsters. Nothing about them was right. Two of them were Latinos. They were after Dennis. I notified the sheriff but there's nothing he could do. What did Dennis do, anyway, make some mafia guy mad?"

"Yes, he did, sir." Cody said. "My partner, here, didn't alleviate matters. By the way, we have to be nameless to you. Sorry, but the same mafia people are after us, also."

The bartender grinned. "What happened?"

Cody looked him in the eyes and held them. "Dennis's life depends upon absolute secrecy here. He did, we did, while assisting the feds in Colombia, shoot up a bunch of cartel members. No one knows this but us and them. They've been on our tails since then. This was about two years ago. It appears

THE CARTELS ERROR: BOOK FOUR OF THE CODY HUNTER SERIES | 21

they might have caught up with Dennis. We've got to find him first and get him out of the country fast."

The bartender nodded. "I'm glad I got to meet you guys, so here's what I know. Dennis went to see a girl in West Virginia whose dad works or used to work in the mines up there. The lady's name used to be Lucy Moore. The town is Cagney."

Leo grinned and shook the man's hand. "I gave forty bucks to the wrong man. I'll make it even with you."

The bartender refused. "What you owe me is the status on Dennis, if you get there on time, let me know. I like the man. He was like a brother. Can you do that for me?"

Cody grinned while they shook hands. "It will be our pleasure. Now, Lucy Moore, is she married to someone else?"

The bartender nodded. "Yes, she married badly. She has a kid and no one knows where her husband ran off to or with whom. Dennis will make everything right for her."

They shook his hand and said their good-byes.

CHAPTER 3

They rode the bus to Cagney. Once out of the bus terminal, they stopped at the first pay telephone where Cody called Nancy. She expressed no emotion when he explained his situation. He said they must try to locate Bob first and make him safe.

Nancy understood. She didn't mind so much for her as she did for Charley. Cody could never leave the house without Charley. Now Charley missed him and didn't play as much as usual. He stayed in her lap and remained fussy most of the time with fat, little fingers in his mouth.

Cody hated himself for hurting Charley. No one knew better than himself that he needed to be home with his son. What his wife didn't realize is that if they could find Bob, it would only be a short while before the cartels' hit men found him and Leo. He knew that finding Bob meant wiping out the force hired to find him. He and Leo not only needed to find Bob, he needed both of them in order to stay alive. Cody's heart felt so heavy that his face grimaced and twisted into pain.

Leo pretended to let that part ride for the moment. At the first break toward finding Bob, he would insist that Cody return home. In fact, he would take it from there without Cody. He said, "I have to report in. Sit down and give me a second."

Cody sat on a curb nearby and rested his new boots on the asphalt. Only an occasional car passed. That's when he caught his mistake. A rental car! The driver, a white male, noticed Cody at the same time their eyes made contact. His three passengers gawked at both Leo and Cody.

Cody cursed himself for his carelessness. As usual, he wore his starched jeans, new boots, and a cheap straw hat whose crease appeared more cowboy than any hat ever creased at the factory. It would take him a week to reach his side arm in his suitcase.

He checked himself. He knew that he needed to be more diligent in order to dodge these people. While searching for Bob, the bad guys now had both Leo and Cody captured. *Nice going, Cody!* He thought.

He rose to his feet and watched the car make a fast U-turn. He now realized a larger mistake by having his gun safely stowed away in his one piece of luggage. He barely had time to call to Leo, who hung up the telephone upon spotting the automobile full of four armed suspects. The guns pointing at him and Leo surely belonged to pure professionals. They appeared out of nowhere and suddenly had them captured at a time least expected.

Cody realized his and Leo's images would have been carried by the hunters as they searched for Bob, who would stand out less telling. He had no time to dive for his small luggage.

The driver stepped out in a jovial mood, his side arm pointed straight and steady at one of their heads, then the other's.

"Well, hello Cody Hunter and Leo! What a pleasant surprise! We've been watching the bus terminal and streets in this red neck city for days, just waiting on you two hillbillies. Now you're here!"

Leo returned his smile. "We don't know you but I'm going to guess you know us through a certain Mr. Albert Luminato. So now you have us but you don't have Bob. That gives us the greatest advantage, Mr. Whatever."

The driver laughed. "I am happy to know you, Mr. Leo. We will have Bob soon enough now that you're caught. You're right about Albert but I think his name is really Alfred."

Leo shrugged. "Whoever, he's going to rot in a federal jail where he and people like you belong."

The driver shrugged as Leo did previously. "Now-now! Let's not be sore losers. Do you know where Bob is located? I'm sure he's in this town or you wouldn't be here. You may answer truthfully. It matters little to you or anyone else right now."

Cody, with his hands lifted halfway with his palms pointed outward, said, "Bob has another name that we gave him. We call him Ghost. He may be watching us as we speak."

The driver believed him. "We don't underestimate him at all, Mr. Cody. However, I think he has a wife and child and is running at this time. If he wouldn't be coming back, then you wouldn't be here. He's somewhere in the city or in the woods right now just to evade us. When we go after him, he will be waiting for us. That's his plan. Do you not agree?"

Cody nodded. "That makes sense. But just in case, let me tell you guys that I wouldn't stand too close together because Bob can and will take you out two at a time with one bullet."

All four men moved to one side to put distance between them. Leo knew at that time that professional people had him in their sights. "For smart men, it sure took you guys long enough to find us."

"Two separate cartels pay us. Instead of giving us a time limit, they pay us unconditionally. They have the money. They also know that we will deliver, sooner or later. It looks good at this time. Our bonus will be astounding!"

"Two separate cartels pay you?" Cody smirked. "Do they pay you too little or too much?"

"Too much, of course!" the driver answered gleefully. "We don't mind. We've been on your trail since you killed the old grey-headed weasel that liked little boys. He was eaten by his own tiger, you know."

Cody nodded. "Only one cat was alive at that time. I put a bullet in the man's head during the attack. He was soiling himself when the tiger attacked. It wasn't frightened at the gunshot at all. Now that you have another fact straightened, let me tell you another. They're paying you far too little. That is, of course, if you don't value you your lives very much."

The driver nodded. "Thanks, but you're wrong. Now let's get back to where it gets tricky. We will expect 100 percent of cooperation from you two. If we don't get it, even by the smallest percentage, you will each get shot in the knee at each mistake you make. You will be alive when you're delivered to your graves, which you will welcome in order to be free from pain. Am I clear on that point?"

"Clear!" they both answered at the same time. "Cooperating is what I do best." Cody said proudly.

Leo followed up with a typical remark. "Do you think that we can stop at a local drug store for a box of aspirin or something? I hate pain."

Cody said, "You'll have our cooperation at its fullest. But I ask you to be fair as in a gentleman's agreement."

The driver nodded. "Ask away. For now, lie down, face down. Put your arms behind your back. Our guns will be pointed at the bend of your legs, the back side of your knees. The handcuffs you will wear will have super glue in them. They will never leave you. In fact, you will be buried in them."

"Clear," Cody answered. "But I asked you for a gentleman's agreement, a professional one. Please don't shoot us in our legs. Our cooperation should mean a little something!"

The driver nodded. "Right now your friend is still running to keep his lady friend safe, along with her kid. So it won't happen soon. We're going to use you as bait in the woods, in a clearing. If he doesn't come within a reasonable time, we'll start shooting one bullet a day into your bodies, for days, if necessary. He will eventually show."

Leo almost chuckled. "Bad idea, sir! He won't show the way you expect him. We might be dead first but he will come when you least expect it, at the airport, in your sleep, while you're eating or at any time. He will come and he will come in a vengeance! My advice to you is to kill us now and run for your lives. There's a downside to this that you don't believe possible. He will find you. I really don't think that you guys know who and what you're up against. I'm telling you now, sir, that you will be safe nowhere on this planet."

They rode peacefully in the back seat of the car with two Colombians sitting on their laps, keeping them immobile and extremely uncomfortable. They drove for an hour and then walked to a clearing in the woods.

The driver spoke. "Leo and Cody, your graves are already dug. You will be chained here until we put all three of you in them. Pictures will be made, voice recordings will be made, blood will be drawn, and you will eat your reasonable choice of foods."

"Big of you!" Leo said. "How would you like us to call you?"

"My name is Bear. The other *gringo* is Horse. These two Colombians are Tiger and Lion. Be reasonable with your requests and you will be made as comfortable as possible until the pain begins. We will take a little pleasure in torturing you, not much. It's pleasure mixed with business. You understand. We will come on the third morning and put a bullet in each of you, in one knee, of course. A bullet in the other knee will follow the next morning, and so on until you are both full of lead. This may sound a bit gruesome but we will endeavor to live with it."

Leo almost chuckled. "You can live with it? Bear, you are terribly ill in this type of humor!"

Bear agreed. "It's a fact. Some facts contain humor, but please try and keep your criticism to a minimum."

Cody chuckled. "You're going to have to eat that one, Leo."

"And by the way, gentlemen, we have many cameras with dates already set, etc. Our superiors will want a complete record of your comments, worries, and, eventually, your cries of pain. Everything will be recorded over the hours or days that you are alive. You will have antiseptics for inflammation and to fight bacteria. Unfortunately, there will be nothing for the pain. You wanted aspirin? Very well, you may have two tablets each day for pain."

Leo grimaced and closed his eyes. "Would it have helped if I had asked for four?"

"No—Mr. Leo, what would have helped if you had not spoken at all. However, without your humor, we might not have thought of aspirin. You may have made my superiors laugh, however. They are hearing everything you say at this very time. They will hear the mosquitos swarm around you whenever they come."

"Let me ask a favor of you, sir." Leo said. "Please let Cody have my two aspirin each day. They thin my blood."

The man who called himself Bear, stopped and stared at them. It became clear to both Cody and Leo that he would be carrying out his mission on his own terms.

"Mm, I doubt if I could do that. Actually, two aspirin might actually help control some of the pain for an hour or so. We don't want that. Pain, you see, if intense sufficiently to suffer around the clock, will help stop your heart from beating. The Vagas nerve will cease delivering messages to your heart. Do you know enough about medicine to know this?"

"Oh—is your real name Doctor Bear?" Leo asked without hesitation.

Cody wished that Leo would stop. But Leo might have a plan and he must put it into action."

Bear stopped and turned in order that Leo could read his face. "I know enough about medicine to know in your particular case that your brain won't allow your heart to stop beating under the worst set of circumstances until many days have elapsed."

"Right you are!" Leo insisted. "You should know this fact, also: All the knowledge in the world cannot change God's mind when He's ready to call us home."

Bear chuckled and turned away. "God calls a man home when a bullet causes the heart to explode. We will inflict the pain, Leo. God will call you home only after we inflict lots and lots of pain over a very long period of time. Otherwise, He might give you another twenty to forty years or more to live."

"Okay!" Leo stated happily. "So long as we're on the same page! Thank you, Doctor!"

Cody frowned at Leo. "Leo, you are such an incredible brown noser! How could any one man be so gifted?"

"Come on, Cody. The sarcasm still belongs in my department. While we're on the subject, Cody, do you know how to pray?"

"Yeah, I know how to pray, Leo. If you have a point, please get to it. My ears want to fall off my head because of you entertainment for our hosts."

"Okay, Cody! Here's my point: Pray, you Arizona heathen! Pray like you really don't want to be tortured to death. Do it for the both of us! I'm going to be doing the same thing, only more for me than you due to your being a heathen and all that."

CHAPTER 4

Two hunters spending their two days off from the mines walked through the woods in search of edible game. They loved the woods. They enjoyed them most when carrying two squirrel rifles and two flasks of Kentucky whiskey. Suddenly, they stumbled upon a man-made clearing and stopped, wondering whether this was a good time to take a swallow from their flasks or not. Knowing to say nothing while practicing their skills for hunting, they waited for a visible explanation.

It never came, the two captured men sat up, partially hanging and sitting with their hands securely chained to a long chain between two posts. Knowing their chances on surprising a squirrel or a deer had suddenly disappeared, they gawked at the two men.

Their hunting luck had just taken a sharp decline. They surveyed the situation further, still daring not to speak. One finally broke the silence. "What in the world are you guys doing out here?"

Both Cody's and Leo's eyes blinked several times.

Then both hunters could not talk fast enough. "Is this a new trick by the game warden to throw us off our hunt?"

Leo, equally surprised as the two hunters, asked, "We just wondered if you were the game wardens."

One of them said, "Then I don't suppose you guys were caught by game wardens. That right?"

"Right," Cody replied. "We were caught by some extremely bad guys that could make game wardens seem like choir boys. We need help but I suggest that you get back into those trees and disappear. Bring help if you can. Please!"

"Why didn't they just kill you outright instead of leaving you out here for the bears and wild cats?"

"They want to make us talk."

One of the hunters scoffed before opening his flask. "About whut? Are you guys with some other union or something?"

"No. We are federal police that got caught by some bad guys that deal in smuggled cocaine." Cody knew they would do nothing until they quenched their curiosity. "We need help if you don't mind."

One of the men chuckled. "You guys are a long ways from home. Ain't no cocaine smugglin' 'round here. Whut're you really doin' here if you ain't scabs or somethin'?"

Leo became more aware of their situation. "We are not scabs! You guys don't have to believe us but you definitely better believe this. You better skedaddle right now before our captors return!"

The bearded one had a long pull from his flask. He nodded affirmatively. "I've heard enough to know whut I'm talkin 'bout. You two yahoos are scabs. Ain't nuthin' else to it. Two scabs caught like fish in a barrel! Now ain't this something for the books!"

Cody said, "We are telling you the truth, sir. We need help!"

"Well, stranger," the smartest hunter said, "I've seen 'em all. We're leavin' but don't 'spect no help from us. You scabs'll git whut you deserve."

Both hunters began to turn when the first bullet arrived slightly ahead of its rifle sound. The first hunter grunted and fell dead with his partner wondering what had happened to his own chest as the second bullet arrived in another large "Whump!" He stared awkwardly momentarily and also fell dead.

Leo shook his head in a tough luck sort of way and said, "Cody, please tell me that the squirrels and wildlife are shooting back during these times."

Dennis, aka Bob, finally breathed easier as the Canadian Port of Entry inspector waved him freely into Canada. For whatever reason, he felt a strong desire to call Dan to report that the boredom that ate his vacation like rain consumes dry soil no longer existed. Usually, if nothing happened, he could see no point in calling. But he wanted to call Dan to see how his partners liked the new situation. This morning, however, personal problems prevailed.

Bob knew of the little time to find their new threat. Something evil had finally creeped into their mist like cancer sneaks into a family. He felt the same way his mother when something wicked seeped into their forest. He protected the only love remaining in his life, the only one he knew. Lucy Moore finally shared a car seat with him after all these years, even if she resented it. He stifled an untasteful derision building in his chest. The new challenge attacked from all directions.

Eating at every instinct stood Lucy, who doubted him. In fact, she didn't seem to care for him at all. She actually wanted to go back home, even after he explained the terrible situation repeatedly. She loved another man. *What fool's role did he attempt with her?* No matter. The real had arrived. He would protect her.

She silently returned his stare as he glanced toward her. What infuriated him most, at himself, not her, she sat blinded from love for some other man. Her man didn't care for her. A gambler, perhaps, who played billiard halls for grocery money. Bob couldn't tolerate the likes of the man but steered clear of Lucy's private love. Her strong resentment tested his limits, but he had to see it through.

The thick trees bore heavy clumps of dark green causing limbs to stretch downward. Their dense odors penetrated his vehicle and seemed to ease the pain of her rejecting his love. Lots of rainfall here, he surmised. This good forest helped keep his planet oxygenated. He fought to feel the goodness to alleviate his burden. *Not working!*

For the first time since the night before, Lucy, smiled meekly in his direction as he looked at her without the anxiety--packed atmosphere they endured for the past eight hours. He felt more gratitude for the trees, for their dark and heavy branches offered hints of security. For whatever reason, he sensed thankfulness for her smile.

She had not seen Dennis is almost four years. She married Lewis after learning that she would be having his baby. By the time their baby arrived, Lewis had abandoned her with no money or a roof over her head. She had no choice but to live with her parents and suffer the indignity her dad put her through at home on his days off from working. Her mother, haggard from living in fear for years, loved her and her child as if she had known no other.

With no advance warning the prior evening, Dennis knocked on their door with his eyes wide and serious. He had no greetings, only a small hug for her mother. He said, "I have little to no time to explain. Lucy, wear what you're wearing and gather what you can inside a minute for the baby. I'll tell your mother what we're doing."

She left his presence without a word but stopped once behind the closed door and breathed. What she knew just happened failed to fully register. Why the sudden rush? Did Dennis want her this much?

Bob looked at Lucy's mother with all the sincerity he knew. "Mrs. Moore, I'm sorry to have to do this. I fear that your's and Lucy's lives are in danger. That probably includes your husband, also. There's a drug cartel in Colombia that has no restrictions on murdering and torturing innocent lives just to annoy their enemy, which is me. My partners and I destroyed one of their farms and damaged another. We claimed a lot of lives. I heard from a reliable source that they are coming for me and the ones I love. I need to get Lucy out of harm's way. Feel free to join us. I have plenty of money."

Mrs. Moore kept her eyes on the floor. "I always wanted you to marry Lucy, Dennis. Just take care of my daughter and her daughter. That's all I ask."

Bob nodded his promise. "They probably know where I am due to my brother in Memphis. He has no doubt given them Lucy's name because she is the only real sweetheart I've ever known. You folks are the people the cartels will want to kill when they want an enemy like me killed. You see, killing me isn't enough. They have to erase my entire existence. Anyhow, if I know my brother, they know that Lucy has a baby and they know she lives with you. That is what I know of my brother. Don't ask, just nod your understanding. God knows that I've never stopped loving Lucy. So they will come. They will kill you and your husband without hesitation if they suspect you know where we are. For this reason, you must come with us. If your husband were here, I would insist on his coming, too."

"Dennis," she said firmly, "I doubt if anyone would kill me and my husband, especially anyone from Colombia. That's just plain dumb! It don't make any sense at all! But have it your way and go on with my Lucy and her daughter. Me and my husband will be just fine!"

Bob took her mother in his arms and hugged her. "Mrs. Moore, I have to save her!"

She looked up at him. "Dennis, I've always known you to be a nice, pleasant man. You wouldn't lie. Yet, you pop in like a stray dog and tell us that our lives are in danger. What do you expect us to believe?"

He gripped her elbows and squeezed them tightly. He dropped to his knees and hugged her waist. "Please, Mrs. Moore! I am C.I.A. I have been to Colombia and we did kill a lot of bad guys. They will spend millions of dollars and millions more to find me and my partners. I have to get Lucy out of their way right now! They know I love her whether we're married or not!"

Mrs. Moore left for a few seconds to return with Lucy carrying the baby. She said, "Stop and feed them, Dennis. Take care of my babies!"

Dennis grabbed her and hugged her while Lucy hugged her. "I will. It may be weeks, but we will contact you again."

They hurried to Bob's rental when Lucy stopped. "Dennis, what in the blue blazes are you doing? This is my life that you're upsetting!"

"Get in the car, Lucy. I know I sound crazy. The bad guys are going to come and they will kill you just to aggravate me! So let me save you and your baby. If your mother will come with us, go get her."

Lucy clung to her toddler daughter. "Momma won't come. She belongs here."

Bob hesitated at the wheel. "I'll not let them have you, Lucy, whether you will ever love me or not, they won't get you!"

With that, he drove away. A day later and now in Canada, she asked, "Will they really kill my momma and daddy?"

Bob concentrated on his driving. "No. I don't think they will right away. They might rough them up a little. It's what they do. But if they're sure they don't know anything, they won't kill them. By my leaving them in Cagney means something and, that alone, tells the bad guys that your parents know nothing."

She hugged her daughter. We need to stop for milk before the stores close somewhere up ahead."

He asked, "You don't breast feed your child?"

"Dennis, how do you know all this? Am I crazy for falling for this craziness? Did the bad guys call you and tell you that they were coming?"

"No. I called my brother for no reason at all and he told me that my friends were looking for me. That's enough to piece together. Then, my old boss called and filled me with their plans. That makes it real, Lucy."

She looked the other way and watched the trees flash by in a blur. Her baby stirred in her lap for a more comfortable position.

"I wish I did breastfeed. I just dried up shortly after she was born."

"What do you call her?" he asked.

"Dolly. Dolly Mullins. Her dad's name is Lewis. We don't know his whereabouts."

Bob nodded. "The sorrier the men are, it seems, the more women love them."

"Not this woman," she said and looked straight ahead.

Bob wanted to say more but kept quiet until he could tell her everything.

He stopped at the first Canadian grocery store. Shafts of bright light filtered through the pines. He walked inside and found a directory. He dialed the home for distressed women. He had thousands in the bank and would spend the last penny on keeping her safe.

She looked at him for the first time without apprehension. "Dennis, so help me, if you're not sincere on this, God will punish you like He's never punished another man!"

CHAPTER 5

As the two Colombians approached with water and food, Cody and Leo both wondered what lay in store for them, an early torture or a totally unexpected miracle from Heaven. Grinning broadly, Leo greeted them as he would any other.

"Good morning, gentlemen! Have you come to give yourselves up?"

Cody grimaced and strained against kicking his partner.

The Colombians checked their chains and showed them a hunting knife to let them know that Leo needed to practice respect.

"We have considered one possible element." One of them said, "I know that neither of you would ever volunteer the information we need, so I am asking with serious desire. One of these two dead hillbillies is your friend, Bob? Is this true? Think! If he is this man, Bob, then we can begin killing you instead of having to wait two more days."

Leo nodded thoughtfully and replied, "We have been contemplating this same thing, brothers. So we believe the answer should be negative since it will induce our torture."

Cody followed up with a different answer. "On the other hand, we figured that you may appreciate truthful and cooperative information from us. So if I may, let me give you the full and truthful story."

The Colombian, not completely confident in his English, looked at his partner and said, "I think a talk from you that is correct truth would be best, *Senor Cody.*"

"Better let me tell 'em, partner." Leo warned.

Cody ignored him and began. "Our careless friend, here, Bob, should have never approached us. We tried to warn him but he had his partner with him. Like I said, he was foolish."

Leo stopped him. "He was our friend! He was not foolish!"

Cody continued. "I am the one who led all the killing of your friends on the ranches in Colombia. It was my wife who was murdered by you cowardly people. One of our friends was shot during this cowardly ambush but the papers said it was me. I do not care. Instead of three men harassing your farms, there were six of us. These two men that you murdered yesterday were a part of the six. You have two more of us. Do not ask us who the other two are because they are of the CIA and FBI. But please note that neither Leo nor our other friend did any shooting. It was Bob and me. That is the truth, my friend. You will have to give me the torture you have planned for Leo."

The Colombian nodded affirmatively and thoughtfully. "You are very brave or foolish for attempting to save your friend, Mr. Leo, from the torture we have planned."

Leo said dryly, "I killed more of your people than Cody or this other man. His name is Felix, but I doubt if that's his real name. I never liked him very much. In fact, I didn't like any of them. I just liked killing you people!"

Both Colombians stared at Leo unbelievably, completely surprised. "You are a very foolish man, Mr. Leo."

Cody scoffed. "Mr. Leo, as you call him, cannot shoot straight. He was better suited at loading our weapons and cleaning them. He is not brave but very foolish."

The Colombian called Tiger agreed and continued. "I think that our friend Bear is going to enjoy getting the real truth from you two men. I do not think that Mr. Leo is very intelligent in his head for thinking."

Cody agreed. He did not look at Leo but continued with his lies. "Bob is the real hero to the American people. I request a proper burial for both men. They did much to keep your cocaine from reaching American shores."

Tiger shrugged. "You think you are correct, Mr. Cody, but they did nothing to stop our cocaine from reaching America in big shipments! Our ranches have earned billions and millions of dollars from the American people who have much love for our cocaine."

Cody looked at the food and found stew meat wrapped in large tortillas. With it came a generous amount of salad. Cody said it seemed enough for two men. Leo agreed and consumed one of the large burros with lots of hot sauce. Cody ate most of his burro and passed the remaining portion to Leo, who made short work of it. He burped and drank tea before settling back against the tree that held the iron post securely.

"So," Cody began using the Italian language as they waited a few moments in silence, "do you have a plan to escape, Leo?"

"Me? Hey, you're the rookie in this outfit. You think of a way out for us. If you don't you won't make probation."

The one called Tiger interrupted them. *"Senores,* please use English in our presence. Another eruption of a foreign language will not be tolerated. "What was that poor representation of Spanish, Portuguese or Italian?"

Leo shrugged. "Italian. It is a very beautiful language, *senor.* You should try and learn it."

Tiger said, "I remember men talking like they heard Italians communicating during a gun fight long ago. That must have been you."

Cody continued in English. "I retired three months ago. I have a nest egg large enough that I could open at least three car dealerships."

Leo thought on the statement a little while and said, "So? You're just going to give up ranching and not own a large cattle ranch or what?"

"No. Ranches are too expensive and cows are too cheap. You're the one that's still drawing wages so you make the escape plans. I'm only a guest."

They both jumped from the new voice behind them. "Lion said uneasily. Who's that? You guys have already had visitors. Who else knows that you're here?"

Cody answered. "There was no need to kill these two men. However, they are escaping torture."

Bear chuckled as he also approached them. "I guess I didn't tell you that we are on a tight schedule. First, you two will kindly bury those men in your graves. You two will have to dig two more, unless you want to double up and share. I don't care. Make it easy on yourselves."

Leo spoke up. "No need of that, boss. We'll let those guys share one and we'll share the other when the time comes."

Bear shrugged. "Suit yourselves. I'd get busy and get some dirt over those guys if I were you. The wildlife may come calling tonight. Keep the knife. You may need it to fight off the bears and big cats."

Leo took a deep breath and said, "Mr. Bear! Before we get into a long dialogue with one another, I'll cut you a deal. You make a fast run into town, call your boss in Bogota and tell him to send you some reinforcements. We'll wait a couple of days in order to make this a fair fight. You'll have your reinforcements and we'll suffer the loss of food and drink for that long. That way, we will both be against fair odds. What do you say?"

A heavy bullet exploded against the ground inches off the tip of Cody's boot. He fired another round at Leo's heel. Leo jumped. "Mr. Bear, please try and be more careful!"

Bear said, "Mr. Leo, I have grown tired of your humor. You pop off just one more time and I'll serve your knee cap right in the center of your dinner plate."

Leo jumped again and said, "You got it, Mr. Bear!"

Bear walked forward a few steps. "Now that we have a more clear understanding, let me say, Leo, that you are a sport! I like that."

Bob drove to the nearest telephone and called Dan.

Dan, their controller, the station chief of the D.E.A. office in Bogota, understood Bob's urgency and broke the news that he had no help to support him and his partners. They would have to fight the mercenaries alone. Afterwards, get back to Colombia and finish the job on the cartels while the Colombian government was still on their side.

Bob then stated that he had no idea of where Leo or Cody might be.

"Okay, Bob. As I said, get back to Cagney, find those mercenaries and find Cody and Leo. Leo called me and said they were in Cagney, then he was just not there anymore. He hasn't called back. He and Cody may be dead or worse, captured. Find 'em!"

Bob spoke into a dead line. "After I make Lucy safe, I'll get right on it."

Dan had beaten him to a fast hang up and sat with a gratifying smile. He said to no one, "Good luck to you, Bob."

Bob stopped in the middle of the road. His stomach tightened and began to burn. What to do? There's only one motel in town. He hoped to find them there. They might be able to rent a car here. That shouldn't be so difficult. He knew the clean cut cowboy and the well-dressed Leo would stand out in Cagney. He doubted if they had the time to find a motel or a car before they got themselves killed or captured by the mercenaries. Either way, he now faced another challenge that he least desired.

Bear grinned as he walked into the clearing. "You know, this is the only problem in taking you guys into the woods for a little privacy and time to do some serious reflection. There are more backwoods people here than wildlife. These guys are locals and both of you know it! They aren't your friends! You think lying and running a bluff like that will get passed me? These dead hillbillies were simply roaming through the trees looking for animals to eat for dinner. They walk these woods like a lady pushing a cart in a grocery store! We're going to have to make some changes before two more stumble upon us. You two start digging some new holes."

"Well," Leo suggested. "You get us some tools and we'll do just that, Mr. Bear."

Bear reflected a second and said, "Well, we have the tools right here for you. If you wear these out we'll get you new ones."

Leo removed his shirt down to the handcuffs and shoved it toward the one called Bear, who cut each sleeve with the knife he carried in his boot.

Bear turned to Cody. "This is going to be difficult. We have a lot of rock outcroppings, so there's rock underneath shallow soil here. Lion and Tiger dug your graves. So you guys dig them deeper and we'll put all four of you in 'em."

Cody lifted a hand toward Bear. "No. We will dig two new graves. That's something to do with respect whether you understand it or not."

Bear looked down at him and agreed. "So long as there's time for respect, you guys got it."

Cody grinned and nodded his head in disbelief. "Bring us some pesticide. We're going to need it after the bodies began to rot."

Bear nodded. "I love cooperation. All this is in your favor, you know."

"I'd like a pick to go with the shovel." Cody said. "Bring him water and gloves, too. We don't want him to have blisters."

Leo looked at him. "Are you crazy? What's a pick, for goodness sakes? I don't understand you, Cody. You hillbilly types have a strange language after you killed off all the good English words."

"A pick-axe, Leo."

"Oh. Why didn't you say so?"

Bear looked at both men with a puzzled frown. "You guys are a little strange."

Leo said, "We don't kill and torture people for a living, Bear. If you don't have the tools, say so. Do you need anymore help with our request?"

"No. We'll return shortly with a pick-axe instead of a crowbar. Horse will be in the trees keeping an eye out for things. Don't do anything that will tick him off. Okay?"

Cody seemed slightly exasperated. "Well, tell him not to stray too far. A stranger to these woods can easily lose his way."

Bear nodded. "One more thing! Are you guys going to keep the noise level down?"

"Noise level? You are the strange one, Bear." Leo answered gruffly. "I'm not going to attract the attention of any feral dogs or other wild animals, if that's what you mean. Don't worry about Cody. He doesn't like to talk, anyway."

Bear grinned and faced them. "Cooperation is good. You know, it's too bad we have to waste you guys. I'm beginning to like you."

Cody spoke up. "I don't get it. We're all American people, here, except your lion and tiger. Instead of staying in the military or finding jobs, you hire out to big money people in Colombia as mercenaries. Doesn't this bother your good side any at all?"

Bear expected this and welcomed his chance to explain. "You kidding me? Man, do you have any idea how much money we're making by doing this? Oh—I know! We're not going to draw much social security when we're old enough but who needs it?"

Cody's face suddenly turned toward Leo, who looked away. "Social Security? Leo, are we paying into that?"

Leo laughed. "Not now, home boy. The OPM is saving money and earning money from the banks where our back wages are located. When we collect, there will be fees and fines galore. Yes, we will pay into it!"

Cody nodded. "We're probably paying insurance that we don't know about, also. Sorry I asked, Leo."

CHAPTER 6

They dug three feet down before they struck limestone stratum. The digging became laborious. Bear and Horse watched with enthusiasm. After Cody and Leo began puffing and sweating profusely, Horse stepped up to the dangerous tools his captors possessed. Bear watched closely with his weapon ready.

"Rest yourselves, men!" he said. "I haven't done this in years. Give me some room, please."

Cody and Leo backed out of the hole and let Horse make heavier and noisier sounds with the pick-axe. "He's good." Cody noted.

"Smart," Leo added. "He's getting in a day's exercise in just a few moments. Bear? Are you going to get in on this?"

"Sure! No hurry, though."

Horse swung a few more times and felt winded. He tossed the tools toward Bear. "Have all you want, partner. There's plenty to go around."

Bear shucked his shirt. Both men obviously worked out in gyms. "I'll last an extra minute more than Horse if you guys want to time me."

Bob failed to find a rental home near the Moore residence. He stopped at a telephone booth and called Mrs. Moore. She admitted to having strange visitors that asked a lot of questions about her daughter but they showed no hostility toward her. They claimed to be looking for Lewis, her husband, whom they claimed owed their casino money. She didn't believe them. She made them out of be exactly what Bob warned her to expect. He needed to be ready for them if they showed up again.

In the meantime he knew nothing else to do. Being a male in his working age didn't seem appropriate to be idle on the street. He walked to the nearest billiard's parlor and found idle men his age sitting and staring at idle tables. He found a chair near a window that allowed him to watch the street.

Two men approached him and asked if he would like a game. He declined. Then they asked what he was doing in the house if he didn't play.

Instead of answering, he stood up and flexed his arms and wrists. "I didn't say that I didn't play, friend. I simply declined your offer to play. Now what is it that you have in mind?"

This caught them both off guard and one half-laughed. "You any good at Eight Ball?"

Bob answered truthfully. He could barely hold a cue stick, far less of playing. "No. I hardly know the game."

They promised to teach him, although their skepticism glared at him. One of them said, "Loser pays for the table."

He chose the nearest stick and looked down the long rod to detect the arcs. "Go ahead and break," he said.

"No." the gentleman said. "We'll vie for the privilege."

Bob watched while his opponent set the heavy white ball in front of him and tapped it. The ball bounced off the opposite side and rolled to a standstill near the side it started. He guessed it to be a winning stop. Nevertheless, Bob tried and his stick bounced off the cue ball.

They laughed. A few more locals gathered in. No one talked. Bob's opponent nodded. "Try again. Only this time, be serious. We're honest folks here."

Bob looked him squarely in the eye. "So am I, friend. To save time by cutting to the chase, I have no intention of playing more than one game with you or anyone else. Now, I'll gladly pay for the table for anyone else to play in my place."

His opponent insisted. "Friend, you'll play the game. Now take a serious shot at beating me to break."

Bob took his time and sent the ball spinning to its left, almost hitting the racked balls. Everyone laughed except his partner, who took the cue ball and set it up for the break. He broke and three balls found side pockets. He grinned. "I play an honest game, mister. You might as well sit down. The game is already mine."

Bob nodded and placed his stick back on its holder and paid the curious clerk for the table. Once that was done, he resumed his position in the chair by the window. His opponent finished the game and walked back to him.

"That wasn't friendly, mister, walking off like that just because I got lucky on the break. How's about a second game? Let's say for five bucks?"

Bob watched two men through the window that left a rental car and walked into a hardware store. They didn't seem to be locals. He turned to the pool shark and said, "No. Thanks for the offer. I thought that I might enjoy playing one game and I found out that I can't even hold a stick right. So, if you'll excuse me, I'll sit here by the window and leave you to your game."

His opponent frowned. "Now, you really are being unfriendly. You have all the ear marks of a hustler. But a good hustler wouldn't make your stupid mistakes, nor would he walk off when I told you that I had won the game, already."

Bob nodded. "I apologize for my offending you or anyone else on the premises. I am new in town and wanted to start off by partaking in a friendly game. I blew it. I'm sorry."

The man nodded and said, "Well, I do believe that you want to be friendly. How about buying a round of drinks for the house? Do that and we'll accept your apology."

Bob looked into his wallet and found a few bills. He looked up and asked the clerk how much for a round of drinks.

The bartender shrugged and looked at the floor for a moment. He looked up and said, "Twelve dollars."

Bob fished out a five and six ones. He shook his head and looked back at his opponent. "I'm short. Care to loan me a buck?"

The pool shark pulled a roll from his pocket and peeled off a dollar. He dropped it on the table next to him. "Now you're obligated."

Bob walked to the table and dropped his eleven dollars on it. He didn't want trouble with this man but it seemed unavoidable. "I'll be back tomorrow about this time or earlier and we'll settle up."

The man nodded. "The interest on a twenty-four-hour loan is five bucks minimum. I'd be here with some cash on you, boy. You also need to know this, too. Punctuality!"

Bob grinned. "Right! I'll be here, God willing. In the meantime, take care of yourself and enjoy the drink on me."

Bob walked in the direction of the hardware store, anywhere to get out of sight of the pool shark and his high-interest loans. He reasoned that it must be difficult for a shark like himself to earn a living in a small town like Cagney.

The clerk in the hardware store relaxed behind the cash register. He watched Bob enter the store and nodded his greeting. When Bob approached him, he knew for sure that something about his last customers had raised suspicion in this friendly stranger as well as himself.

He asked, "Did those men know anything about the courtesy between travelers and hosts."

The clerk denied knowing them. "They struck me a little strange. I seldom sell digging tools to anyone in town since the company pays for all shovels and pickaxes. They paid cash and failed to tell where they lived or what they planned to do with the tools. They didn't speak the local language and raised suspicion of being up to just no good. They had none of the simple politeness one sees around here."

"They left on the east road out of here. Is that right?"

"I assume so. Who are they? Do you know them?"

Bob answered negatively and waited another minute for the sake of good manners in the event the clerk wanted to ask another question. He drove the same street out of town that the strangers had taken.

CHAPTER 7

Bob drove slowly. With no other cars on the road until a shift change, he disrupted no traffic after studying each turnoff, a little thing he learned from Cody, who told him that tracking cars posed no problem once they left the asphalt. Most roads led to houses. He spotted no car resembling the one parked in front of the hardware store.

He drove ten miles further and found several small roads leading off the highway but only two sets of fresh tracks. He kept driving until he reached a larger town that had an airport. The only man on the premises seemed happy to oblige Bob with a rental. However, without a license, Bob would have to hire a pilot, which cost the same as the airplane rental. Flying over the treetops and following side roads seemed a bit unusual to the pilot but he kept his questions to a minimum.

"I'll have to be paid daily, you know," the pilot reminded him. Hard cash works best but I'll agree to a credit card.

"I'll pay your price. You're only trying to earn a living like the rest of us."

"So when do we start?" the pilot asked.

"Right now," he answered. "I hope you've done the preflight."

"Not to worry, sir! We'll take the little one, here. It burns less gas."

"Will it keep the two us in the air in this humid weather?"

"You bet! The lady I'm teaching to fly weighs as much as you and we do all sorts of stalling techniques in this humidity. What are we looking for, anyway?"

"Campers," Bob answered. "Small cabins with a white luxury sedan parked by it. Anything out of place, if you will."

The pilot shrugged. "You got a lot of area to look at, man. We'll fly by the lakes first."

Bob corrected him. "Let's fly the side roads first."

"Whatever! It's your dime. Can you keep one of these little guys in the air? If so, you can fly and I'll ride. That way you'll go exactly where you want and when."

Bob declined the offer. Flying scared him. He hoped that this pilot didn't like to crash airplanes as well as Cody.

They checked both sides of the highway and found nothing resembling a camp with a white car. The trees seemed extra green from the top with a dark brown soil underneath them. A green and brown color, Bob noticed, a rich soil and healthy trees. He gave up looking and asked the pilot to circle the lakes. They found nothing suspicious at any lake. The pilot asked if Bob had enough time in the air. Bob thoughtfully nodded affirmatively. He couldn't think what to do next.

That night, at the motel, he thought that he had used up his ideas. He called Mrs. Moore again and reached Mr. Moore instead.

"You the one called Dennis?" he asked with no attempt to hide his contempt.

"I am, sir. I am…"

"What the hell have you done with my daughter? She's married, you know!"

"Settle down, Mr. Moore! We need to talk. The men..."

"You listen to me, Mr. Dennis or whatever your name might be! I..."

"I'm only going to say this once, so listen up!" Bob used his strongest voice against the man who could get tough with women but bluffed most men. "You and your wife are in serious danger from the men who came by to ask about Lewis and his wife. They..."

"I'll hear none of your tough talk, Mr. Dennis. If you think you're man enough, come on by the house, night or day, and we'll see..."

Bob hung up the telephone and waited a couple of minutes before trying again. Perhaps the man would settle down or let him talk with his wife. He dialed and waited. One the third ring, Mrs. Moore answered. Before he could say more than one word, she said, "Why, hello, Stella! How are you?"

Bob talked fast. "Mrs. Moore, if those men return, run from the house or hide. They will be desperate to find Lucy and myself and they will use knives or guns on you and your husband!"

"Where are you, honey? How was your move to Richmond?"

"Watch for them, Mrs. Moore, or go to a neighbor's house and stay there for three or four days. Those guys will get impatient."

"I know, dear. They're fine. The baby is growing so fast! I don't remember Lucy growing like this. How's your little ones. Are they in college there in Richmond?"

"Mrs. Moore, I left your daughter in good hands in another city far from here. The government has her and the baby in a safe house. She will contact you after I get back to her that the coast is clear. They will kill her if they ever find her. They'll do it just to get at me whether they find me first or not. I'm going to try and talk to your husband again. If I can't, be prepared to lose him."

He hung up while she said good—bye to her friend, Stella.

This time he waited five minutes before calling back. Mrs. Moore spoke and heard Bob's voice. "It's for you, dear."

"Hello!" the gruff voice sounded.

Bob said, "You are in danger of being killed! Now listen to me..."

"I'm gonna call the sheriff! He'll send a deputy over there to your motel and throw you in jail, you worthless pile of monkey dung!"

Bob hung up and quickly snatched his unpacked suitcase and left the motel. Mr. Moore would talk to the mercenaries voluntarily only seconds before they shot him and his wife. He had no choice but to park on the street near their house and wait.

Cody leaned against the damp earth that he removed earlier that afternoon. He pushed the two hunters over the edge and they toppled to the bottom, striking the hard bottom of the graves. Sharp rocks permeated the dirt that lay over the two men.

He wondered if he could sleep under the stars as easily as he had in the past so close to the fresh graves. He felt a chill in the air. With his shirt sleeves gone, he would need cover. If it rained they would need shelter and sound bedding. *"No good!"* he thought. *"Leo will turn into a complaining old hen the moment he slips out of his comfort zone."*

Sounds of the night filled the air that moved silently through the trees. Owls and smaller birds called to one another to keep track of their own species. Without the threat of rain and with a mummy bag, this would be ideal sleeping conditions.

"Hey, Cody, you asleep?"

"Why, yes, I am. Is that you, Leo?"

Leo chuckled from a few feet away. "These guys are lousy hosts. Do you even have an inkling of an idea in how we're going to slip out of this mess that you led us into?"

"It was careless of me to be sure. But I was relying on you."

Leo grinned. *"Of course you were!* We're going to have to jump them. You know that, don't you?"

"No. Don't start anything, Leo. There's always a gun or two on us from the brush. They're fast and accurate. We're going to have to depend upon Bob."

"Bob might be dead, Cody. I know he ain't but when you start depending upon someone else, you're going to lose."

"We are not going to lose, Leo. I've got a little boy at home that likes me. I'm his only dad. You're going to have to come up with something worthwhile instead of jumping them. We're chained to a post as well as handcuffed. We simply cannot afford such handicaps."

"Cody, get this straight because I dislike having to repeat myself. We will jump them when the time is right. Accept it!"

"When the time is right, you say. Very well but I still suggest that you come up with something else, Leo."

"Okay. Let's wait a few hours and test our tethering post for strength and durability. You should be a master at escaping by this time, Cody. I mean, you get captured twice as many times as Bob and I."

"Thanks, pal. I could use a good compliment."

"Go to sleep and dream about how you are not going to make probation on this job, Cody."

Bob drove a city block of where the Moore residence stood among company houses. If they came back, he might stand a chance on getting to them first. He looked up and saw clouds building to blot out the stars, then the moon.

He would wait until around five in the morning and wake Dan. He needed to know where Leo and Cody might be. But taking a chance on calling him wasn't too smart if they had the station bugged.

He waited ten minutes and stared at the empty street. Nothing. No lights except a street lamp at the end of each block. He grinned at the thought of coal mining owners. *Big spenders!* He felt drowsy. He shifted his weight in the seat and drove around the block. He couldn't afford to sleep.

Shortly before Midnight, the telephone in the Moore house rang. Mr. Moore picked it up. "Yeah? Is that you, Lucy?"

Mrs. Moore straightened up and listened intently. She shrank from fright at her husband's response to the caller.

"No! I ain't heard from Lucy or nobody else, you stupid freak! Stop calling my house in the middle of the night! Me and my wife don't know where she's at! You got that? You don't have the sense of that man that came and got her. I asked him where she was and he wouldn't tell me...Yeah, I think he's at the motel...Dennis!...No—I don't know any last name...There ain't anywhere else he can stay but the motel in this town! Now bug off and stop pestering me and my wife!"

Mrs. Moore's eyes flooded with tears. She should have warned him to not tell them anything about Dennis. If they killed him, Lucy might be lost forever. Her husband, always the fool with a loud mouth could get the both killed. She thought of Dennis, knowing that he cared. The criminals definitely wanted Lucy. She waited until he snored and dressed herself.

Bob wanted to go back to the motel and sleep. He had no idea how he would stay awake the next day unless he drove to another town and slept. He could not protect the Moores if they refused to listen. He needed help. *Where are Leo and Cody?*

CHAPTER 8

A light peppering of raindrops woke Cody and Leo. Cody straightened and looked at his watch. One A.M. He felt Leo's elbow bump his shoulders.

"Are you awake, Cody?"

"Yes, unless you're just a bad dream, I am. You seem to have stopped your snoring. Are you going to shower off a bit?"

"I don't snore. Are you going to dig up the tethering post or not?"

Cody tried to reach the shovel handle and failed. He suggested that Leo try. Leo couldn't see it in the dark. Cody tried with his foot and still failed. He straightened up and walked around Leo. The dragging of the chain handcuffed to him scraped against the main line of cable. He leaned against the top of the post and it budged at bit.

Leo helped him and the post loosened a great deal. Since it was nothing but a large six by six post freshly buried, it would slip right out. Leo wrapped his arms around the post and lifted. It came up an inch and stopped.

"What the heck?" Leo grunted.

Cody tried and it stopped solid after he hefted it an inch. "Smart boys!" he whispered.

Leo tried again and it stopped solid. "What do you mean by calling them smart boys? How come this thing doesn't come all the way out of the ground?"

"Simple." Cody answered. "The post is anchored by a long bolt or a rod of some type to keep it from coming out. They dug the hole wide enough for an eye-bolt to screw into it and shoved a big rock on the top of it, then filled the hole with other rocks. I thought I heard them crunching against one another while we loosened the post."

"Okay," Leo said, "What do we do about that?"

Pull the post to where it stops and we start loosening it again. It will be a slow process but it can be done."

Leo shrugged and said, "It stopped raining. The ground is wet, so let's give it a try."

They worked the top back and forth and the post slipped up another inch.

"It's working." They both said and began working the post's top each way the second time. A moment later they had to rest.

Leo said, "Let's try again."

They pulled it up again and the rocks gave way. The heavy post fell and they began working their tethering cable over the top of the long post. Just as they reached the top, three flashlights came on from only ten feet away.

"Congratulations!" Bear said. "If you make one move toward the trees, Horse will cut you down with his full automatic. Or he might decide to use a machete on you. At any rate, you'll be too crippled to walk by the time he's through."

Cody turned to him, still panting heavy. "Don't you guys ever sleep?"

Bear chuckled. "We were asleep. The boys in Bogota had their ears on and heard you with those highly gained mikes on the trees. They can hear you breathe, talk, move, or whatever. I thought I made that clear to you. Anyhow, they called us at the motel and here we are."

Cody accepted the fact and sat down on the damp earth. "We're caught again. I don't suppose that you'd offer us a tarp or something to protect us from the rain?"

"We can do that. We'll dig another hole or two for the posts and string wires between them. We'll throw a tarp over them and you'll have some protection from the elements."

"We appreciate it. Of course, we'll do the work while we're handcuffed. Right?"

"Yes. I'll allow you to do the work. We'll spare a couple blankets for warmth if it rains again. But...the thing of it is, you attempted escape. That's a no—no."

Horse passed his light to someone else and came forward with a small club. In the half light, his speed and hard blow caught Leo's head at the back with a loud thump, causing Leo to grunt and topple forward.

Cody's knees bent slightly as Horse swung and he easily ducked and kicked hard against the midsection of Horse. At that time, a man tackled him from behind and another pounced on his shoulders and head. They waited a few seconds for Horse to recover, which he did with a vengeance. He kicked Cody's ribs and stomped his handcuffed hands. They turned him over and

Horse struck him several times in his face with the club. Cody lay still with his hands paining him. His nose may have been broken and his mouth filled with blood.

He moved his tongue against his teeth. He found one far too loose, broken at its root. He prepared himself for a lot of pain.

"Let me spit!" he said with his voice strained from pain.

They moved and allowed him to empty his mouth.

Bear kicked the soles of Cody's boot and asked, "Are you okay? Would you like to challenge Horse again or is this sufficient punishment?"

Cody nodded. "I'm good, thanks!"

"You'll need to swallow some antibiotics."

"Never mind!" Cody managed to say.

"Oh--but I insist! You aren't going to get infected on us. Swallow it! You can spit later."

Cody obeyed. He looked at Horse's outline. Horse shined the light on his own long face and grinned broadly. "Here I am if you want some more, tough guy."

Cody nodded. "Give me a couple days. Let's keep it between us and let's do it in the daylight. Keep your club and leave me handcuffed. We'll see who ends up with loosened teeth, *tough guy!*"

Bear touched Cody's shoulder. "We make the rules around here. Keep your wants and needs to yourself. By the way, you're getting off easy. I like to shoot people's knees. Horse likes to mutilate victims with machetes."

Cody nodded in the light. "Just as long as your victims are tied, I take it."

Bear chuckled but not from humor. "A smart mouth has gotten more people into trouble than anything else. I dare say that you will regret those words. Horse wants to deal with you now. But you still have two days before I turn him loose on you with a machete. In the meantime, I suggest you use a restrainer on that tongue of yours if you want to have it in your mouth by the time we bury you."

"Alive?" Cody asked.

"Well, yes! I think it's safe to say that you will barely be alive, somewhat. You will have the presence of mind to know that you will die in your grave after you are buried. Think about it. You will be conscious as we shovel the dirt on your face. It will be the last part we cover. You will be allowed to cough and sputter as we toss the dirt slowly, but you will welcome the suffocation. Believe me, you will welcome death."

Bob awoke the next morning thinking that he would keep his date with the local tough guy at the pool hall. First, he had to find a bank and acquire more pocket change. If he could turn that man, two or three more might follow. He needed help. He would also call the Mrs. Moore and ask her if she would consider staying at a motel until this mess passed. He needed call Dan in Bogota first.

Dan had heard nothing from Leo or Cody. He knew they caught the bus to Cagney but that was all. Bob hung up without another word and walked outside.

He called the Moore's house. Mrs. Moore, who had spent the remainder of the night in the tool shed made it back to bed without her husband being the wiser. She started to answer the telephone but her husband beat her to it.

"Lucy?" he asked without saying hello.

"It's me, Dennis," Bob said. "Don't interrupt, Mr. Moore, please! You've got..."

"I beg your pardon, Mr. Dennis. I'm a little tired of you, especially after you kidnapped Lucy away from our home. I want her back here, now!"

"I'll get her back to you, Mr. Moore, after this mess is over, but first..."

"I want it over now, Dennis! You got that? Your friends called again last night and woke us up. I told them to talk to you. I assumed you were at the motel..."

Bob almost shouted at him. "Those men are out to kill Lucy in order to get at me! They will kill you and Mrs. Moore if you don't listen to me! Now please allow me to talk!"

"I think you're full of crap, Mr. Dennis. Nobody is going to kill anybody. You're making all this up while you're trying to keep Lucy for yourself. Well, I'm getting the sheriff on you for kidnapping! Do you think you can understand that?"

"Yes sir, I do understand that. Can I please talk with Mrs. Moore?"

"No! When I get my hands on you, I'm going to beat you to into the bloody mud, Mr. Dennis! Think about that!" He slammed the telephone down without allowing Mrs. Moore to talk.

He needed help to watch the Moore house on Seventh Street. He drove to the House of Billiards and hoped to find Leo playing but he knew wishful thinking sometimes meddled with his mind.

The leader stood up and welcomed him. In fact, they shook hands.

"First of all, my friend, you owe me six bucks. Do you want to pay me now or shall we play double or nothing?"

Bob pulled a five and a one from his pocket. He placed both bills on the nearest table. He asked the brazen man his name.

"Me? Everybody knows my name around here. It's Hook. Why? Are you curious about who's gonna make you go home without any money in your pocket? He grinned broadly.

Bob nodded and said, "My name is Bob. I'm from Memphis. I don't play much pool, never have."

Hook said, "We're glad to know you, Bob. I have never met a man from Memphis that doesn't play pool. What's your reason for not following a great American tradition?"

My dad was a preacher and he didn't allow me to learn the game. So I lost interest in it after I started dating girls."

A couple of men among four chuckled at Bob's reason for not playing pool. Bob's face remained stable.

He said, "Now that I've paid my debt, I want to know if you've seen a couple of strangers in town. One is short, heavy built red headed guy. The other looks like a cowboy, hat and boots, you know."

Hook asked him, "Are you a cop?"

"Noo! I'm an insurance adjuster. The pair in question doesn't have anything to do with insurance but the redhead married my sister in Memphis about six months ago. He left her without saying bye or anything. He claimed to be a good friend of Lewis Mullins who lives here in Cagney."

One of the men in back spoke up. "Maybe he don't like ladies anymore."

Bob nodded slightly. "Really? I don't like maybes. Mr Hook, will any of you guys help me?"

"Maybe!" Hook spoke up. "We know Lewis. He left town. He left a little sparkle behind who dropped a kid since he left."

Bob knew that Hook used the word maybe just to irritate him, since he used it twice with emphasis on it. Bob grinned.

"The abandoned lady is my sister. What's with the good old boy thing that abandons women after they marry them?"

Hook shrugged. "Maybe they just like cowboys better. Who knows?"

Bob said, "Okay. I'll be going. Have you guys seen any strangers at all lately?"

Hook stepped forward to block his way. "Don't be in such a rush, Bob. Stick around. We might even let you buy us another round of drinks. What do you say to that?"

Bob's grin broke into a broad smile. "No thanks, gentlemen, I have to be going. It's going to be a busy day."

Hook didn't budge. Bob didn't like the man and hoped that Hook would press him a bit further. But as he walked around, Hook remained steady and saved his nose and lips from a serious bruising. Bob drove to the Sheriff's Office. He didn't like to have the attention of the police but Leo and Cody, being strangers, might have broken a rule. That would land them in jail.

CHAPTER 9

Bob failed to find his partners in jail. In fact, no officer present knew of their presence in Cagney. None were aware of any other strangers in town. Satisfied with that department, he turned to leave when he noticed Mr. Moore sitting in the sheriff's office. He recognized the face that had aged a bit since he last saw him when he attended Lucy's high school graduation. He paused near the door where he could face the man.

A deputy passed him and wanted to be helpful. "That man is Tommy Moore. He works at the mines and is a good man. If he's visiting the sheriff on business, someone is in serious trouble."

Bob nodded, "I know him from years ago. I dated his daughter in her senior year in high school, although we lived across the world from each other."

The deputy shook his head sadly. "She's married to Lewis Mullins, a no good thief that couldn't hold a job at the mines. He just upped and left her cold after he made her pregnant."

Bob nodded and gave the man a sad smile. Women seem to love men like that."

"Well, not all of them. My wife told me that she was proud of me."

Bob smiled and gave the man a pat on the shoulder. "You've got a keeper, my friend."

"I'd better! We got a set of twins. Oh—here he comes. I'll stick around to see if he recognizes you."

Tommy Moore locked eyes with Bob and held them. He squinted and paused before he pointed a finger at him. "That's him, Lou, that's Dennis, the man who kidnapped my daughter!"

The sheriff walked swiftly around Moore and stopped before Bob. "Is that true, son? Did you kidnap Tommy's daughter?"

"No—sir! I did no such thing. I did take her to a safe place where she wouldn't be killed on account of me. I would've also taken Mrs. Moore, too, but she wouldn't leave her husband."

Tommy Moore rushed forward and grabbed Bob's shirt. "Where did you take her? Where is she?"

The sheriff pushed Moore back and took hold of Bob's arm. "You'd better have a seat in my office. Tommy isn't the sort to make up stuff against anybody. You're going to have to explain your actions, son."

Bob nodded. "That's exactly what I came here to do, Sheriff, because I need your help. Mr. Moore, here, is going to get himself and his wife killed if they don't open their minds."

Moore rushed Bob again, this time knocking him against the friendly deputy, who stood awkwardly in place.

Settle down, Tommy!" the sheriff ordered. "If you don't I'll be locking you up, too!"

Bob kept his hands at his side and followed the sheriff inside his office. "I'll explain myself, sir. First, there are mercenaries here that are out to hurt me. They will start with Lucy if they can find her and then they'll hurt me by killing Mr. Moore, who has, thus far, refused to listen to me."

The sheriff said swiftly. "You're seconds away from being locked up, so I wouldn't be making any threats if I were you, buddy!"

Bob started to deny the threat, but he needed to remain a free man. "I'm sorry, sir. I've been trying to talk sense to Mr. Moore but he refuses to listen. I need help, sir."

The sheriff settled Moore into a chair further across the room. "Now! You have my attention but you had better start making sense instead of blabbing something paranoid."

Bob used his bogus C.I.A. credentials and explained what he and his partners had done to the cartels outside Bogota. He said they had hired mercenaries to find all officers responsible and kill their loved ones first. He leaned back and eyed Tommy Moore coldly.

The sheriff said gruffly, "Lucy Mullins ain't a loved one to you, sir. She married another man and has a child by him."

"Begging your pardon, sheriff, she's a loved one to me, and the mercenaries know it. I can thank my brother in Memphis for that. Maybe she does feels different, being married and all, but I don't. The mercenaries learned from my brother in Memphis that I was in love with her after all these years and have forsaken all others. He even told them what town she lives in. The mercenaries don't care about anyone and they go out of their way to kill the loved ones of their enemies. That's the way the cartels exert their revenge. They kill the families first."

"How many years have you known her?" the sheriff asked.

"Fourteen. She didn't want to marry me and leave her parents. I joined the army and left. I didn't get over her. I passed some tests and became a member of the C.I.A. I visited her frequently for at least ten years. During this time three of us agents went to Bogota and cleaned up two small cartels by killing most of them outright. The C.I.A. will deny this, so you don't need to check. It made the back page headlines over here, but it made big news in Bogota. The head honcho of one cartel kept jaguars in cages. Occasionally, he fed them a man. You may have heard of that."

"Yeah, I heard about it and thought it was all *crapola*. It still may be as far as I'm concerned."

"Suit yourself, Sheriff, but it's a fact. I have two partners up here somewhere. They followed me here and I fear the mercenaries have them. They're probably driving a white rental Chevrolet. My two partners are out of touch and I cannot find a trace of them. This is why I need your help."

"Do you have anyone that I can call to verify all this baloney?"

Bob gave him Red's number in D.C. My name is Bob Ferguson. The man you will call is named Red. Tell him who you are, where I am, and how I look. You will go through two receptionists before you reach him, if you reach him at all. He will deny being C.I.A. and claim U. S. Customs, as will the receptionists. Please be patient with them."

The sheriff took a long breath and let it out. "I ain't making no long distance calls on this telephone!"

Moore leaned forward. "He's lying, Lou. Make 'im tell the truth and make 'im tell me where my daughter is at."

The sheriff looked at Bob questionably. "Tommy is making sense, son. Perhaps you'd better tell us where Lucy is."

"I will not do that. She is hidden safely and that's where she's staying until I have those mercenaries under control."

The telephone rang. The deputy answered and reported to the sheriff. "This is Mrs. Roberts. She said a car pulled in front of the Moore's house and two men got out. She saw them! In a little while she heard a gunshot and the men walked from the house, got into a white car and left."

Bob got to his feet. "I have my own car. Those two men may have murdered my men and I'm going after them."

Moore rushed at Bob and pointed his finger at his nose. "You better hope that my wife is okay, Dennis. If she ain't, I'm going to kill you with my bare hands!"

The sheriff said, "Donald, take Tommy with you. I'm going with this so-called spook agent, here. I have a radio. Notify me if Mrs. Moore ain't okay. And Tommy? You shut your mouth right now! Don't get in Donald's way."

Bob sped to the Moore house. On the way, he talked to the sheriff. "Sir, I need to know which direction that white car went. Point Mrs. Roberts out to me so I can ask her. Now I'm telling you this for a reason. These men mean business. Mrs. Moore is already dead. I'm sure of it. These men have my partners. They may be still alive because they're going to use them for bait to get at me. Then all three of us are dead. You really don't need you to go with me. If you do, be forewarned that these people aren't scared of any law, army, or anyone. They will kill anyone because they simply like to kill people. They know how to fight and ambush. If you don't keep Mr. Moore under lock and key, they will kill him, too!"

The sheriff said nothing but listened. "I'm not letting you out of my sight! That's Mrs. Roberts on the right side of the street telling those ladies what happened."

Bob honked his horn and sped to her. He braked even with her and asked. "Mrs. Roberts, which way did that white car go?"

"Straight ahead. That's all I know!" she shouted.

Bob gunned the rental and hoped he had the right road. The white car had minutes on him. "Where does this road lead to, sheriff?"

"The mines."

Bob slowed. "We're going the wrong way!"

He checked each intersection for tire tracks that left rubber on the asphalt.

Minutes later, he found the tracks turning left. He followed.

"How do you know those skid marks weren't made by a kid driving his daddy's pickup?"

"I don't but it's the only game in town. Where does this road lead us?"

"It leads to its end at an old mine that's closed."

Bob slowed and turned around. The sheriff looked at him puzzled. "I thought that you wanted to catch those guys."

"No sir! You don't chase these guys to catch them. If they think a car is following them, one or two will jump out and ambush the chaser. The driver and passenger will never see them. If they turned off toward that abandoned mine, then I'm positive of an ambush, which is why they made a hit in the daytime, to get someone, law officers or not, to follow them. But it's me they want. If we follow that car, we'll both be killed."

The sheriff looked at him suspiciously again. "You know something? You are one suspicious man. Tell me how you're going to catch them."

I plan to leave my car about a mile short of the turn off and walk into the forest. If I find them, I'll ambush them."

"What if they're not the killers?"

"I'm not kill crazy, sheriff. Now, tell me exactly how far up the road does it end?"

"I really don't know, exactly." The sheriff said. "We'll have to get a map."

Bob gunned it again and sped back to the station. He waited five minutes and grew more fidgety. He thought about hiking in alone but he needed the sheriff or a deputy to drive his car back to the station. Inside he saw Tommy Moore bent over a chair sobbing. The sheriff patted his shoulders.

"Tommy, they're going to shoot you, too. I've got to lock you up so we can keep an eye on you."

"Let them try to come and get me!"

"Hush and get on in there. We'll take care of you."

"It should've been me, Lou. She didn't do anything to anybody!"

He cried again as he walked to the cell. "Oh—my God. Why her?"

CHAPTER 10

Bob knew that he should call Lucy right away but she would only walk away from the safety of the shelter and be killed at her mother's funeral. It was a dirty thing to do but he had to keep her and her child safe.

The sheriff came to him with a map after he locked Tommy Moore in a cell. "You know something, Dennis? The man wants his daughter. She needs to know what happened to her mother."

"I'll call her. But I cannot allow her to come."

"It ain't your decision, Dennis. I'm assuming that's your name. Something else, too, while I'm at it. I'm calling the F.B. I. in on this. If you don't produce Lucy, and fast, you're going to be looking at some serious jail time."

Bob felt robbed. He looked at the floor. He put his hand on the sheriff's shoulder and said. "If you call them, Lucy will come and she and her daughter will be shot just like her mother. They may not care about Tommy, but women and kids are their primary targets. Let me use your phone for a collect call to D.C."

Red listened to Bob as he reported the latest happening. "How sure are you about this abandoned mine. Are you sure that's where they're being held?"

"It's the best shot I have, sir. It makes sense. All the other roads are well traveled."

"How about the kids? Don't the kids use this road to park and smoke pot?"

"I assume they do, Red. The mercenaries won't be in the mine but somewhere near it. I'll be going in on foot in order to find it. Now, look, the sheriff, here, is threatening to call the FBI. I can't afford to be interviewed by them while Leo and Cody are still missing. I need you to call in a favor from the F.B.I. Don't let them come here until I'm finished with the mercenaries."

"Can't do that, Bob. I'm sorry. Try and postpone the funeral a few days. That may give you enough time to bring this mess to a close."

"I'll try, boss. I'm sorry that I by-passed Dan to get to you, but the F.B.I. scares me. We may get knee deep in this, boss, since local law enforcement are in on this and have access to me."

Red sighed. "No. You will be caught and maybe the other troopers, too. I have to remind you. You'll take this fall by yourselves and leave me and Dan out of it. That's the deal."

"That's what I meant by using the word *we*. That didn't include you and Dan. I'm sorry. We're men of our word."

Bob found the sheriff waiting. "Are we going to dump you out there?" the sheriff asked.

"I am leaving you to drive my rental car back here in the event something happens to me. Give me two hours. I'll return with my two partners. That's the plan.

The sheriff was still skeptical. I overheard part of your conversation. What did you say your boss's name was, Red?"

"That's it for today and tomorrow. They'll change the code from U.S. Customs to something else in a day or two. I need water and a sandwich. I'm ready to go for that hike."

Bob walked passed the small road leading to the mine. As expected, empty liquor bottles and beer cans littered the road. Young people would have their kicks just like their parents and their parents before them. He swung to the left and began looking for car tracks before the sun dropped behind the tall sugar pines.

He walked toward the mine and found no part of a road. He walked back to the main road leading into town. He felt frustrated and helpless. He knew that time was short, that these people waited on no one. The wanton murder of Mrs. Moore told him that they were on their way out. If they had Leo and Cody, they would leave their carcasses exposed.

Cody also knew that time was running out. Leo grew quieter and more sullen. Being locked up numbed a personality, especially one like Leo's. Anger built inside him like a volcano slowly growing active. Leo walked out of one jail and had his liberty robbed again before he really had time to debrief himself. Like a man that became useless, he sat in silence and stared at nothing in front of him. He repeatedly picked up a small stone and flipped it beyond his feet.

He nodded negatively and uttered a few words barely discernable. "I guess we've had our go of it, partner."

Cody sensed life in the man as he felt himself slowly beginning to give up. It pleased him to know that Leo would still talk. He needed encouraging. He needed to know they had many capers remaining. "Bob is close, Leo. I feel it."

"He ain't close, Cody. Don't try psychology on me. We've had our time in the fast lane. All it took from us was one small mistake. We are buying the farm, old partner. We have had some good times, but it all came to a head when you screwed up."

Cody kept life in his voice. Leo didn't mean his last sentence. He still had his humor. "Leo, I've lost count of the times I've screwed up. You and Bob carried me past a few danger zones that I know I wouldn't have lived without you two. Thank you. Now--what I really want to know is this, are you going to continue to cry like some old woman that just buried her sixth husband? If so, please allow me to go first."

Leo's voice showed more signs of life than before. "Well, if you insist, I'll tell 'em to shoot you first every time. I'll do you that one last favor."

Cody grinned. "You've lost count of time. We have one more day left before they shoot us. They'll come in the morning after tomorrow. Besides, you just talked like I'm a partner. I'm no longer on probation. Right?"

Leo sniggered at that. "Cody, you're naïve. If by some miracle we skate on all this, rest assured that you will still be on probation for at least three more years."

Cody said, "By the way, Leo. If and when the time comes for us to be shot, we'll jump them and make them kill us fast."

Leo scoffed. "Oh—sure we will! I'll jump them and you'll run for the trees while they fill me full of bullets."

Cody shook his head sadly and smiled. Leo would die with his humor. He said, "I'll lead the charge for the two of us, Leo. You have my word."

Leo stretched and yawned. "Ah--I don't think so, Cody. I'm not so sure that I can handle all those guys by myself. You might decide to throw your hands up in the heat of battle and surrender. I'll be left holding the bag."

Cody chuckled. "Of course you're right. It would never happen if you and Bob would let me make probation, but you won't. I know that. You're both just naturally unfair. But when our noses finally touch the grindstone, like it is now, you get all despondent and pitiful sounding. Whatever happened to 'Never give up?' You seemed to have lost your sense of humor, Leo. You seem all desiccated as life has slowly begun to drain from your body. You're sweating because you know that you're too young to die, but you ain't. You've had it, old son. I don't blame you for giving up. Personally, I have a feeling that I'm going to make it. But I'll loan you my handkerchief if you want to cry a bit. Is your heart slowing down, Leo?"

Leo scoffed again. He loved morbid humor. "Don't even try to tell me that I'm giving up, you worn out old pair of an old maid's bloomers. I don't give up. I have real Irish blood in me!"

Cody's voice also came to life. "Hey—I'm the real Irishman of this outfit! You're only Boston Irish. I have more Irish blood in me than an auditorium full of you Boston phonies!"

"Not so loud, Cody! Remember they have microphones all around us. You're giving them what they want." Leo switched to Italian. "The iron bus leaves Rhode Island in red underwear! Your grandmother's skirts are two sizes too large!"

Cody laughed. He responded in Italian: "Ah--donkey's dung! You are a little bug. You are an old spider that lives under the porch of a policeman's outhouse. You eat the flies off sewer's filth."

Leo laughed louder. "My babies are Nazi criminals and they are coming to free us tonight after it's dark but before the sun goes down!"

Cody began to laugh again in spite of his broken tooth. His entire head began to pain him as he thought about it. "I know that your alligator's back teeth chomped a freight train in half before it loaded Colombian tacos full of worms."

"We must not talk in code, my rich brother of a Bogota whore! Save your money for a chicken fried steak in Altas, Oklahoma."

"Yes!" Cody agreed. "We will keep our captors' entertained by talking like Texans. The cigarette is lighting the London Bridge in New York City!"

Leo responded in Spanish. "Good night, my good friend!"

They both closed their eyes drifted into sleep knowing that cartel members would bring in interpreters from the university tomorrow only to become frustrated.

Bob flew the area early the next morning. Time seemed to dwindle too fast. They found nothing that resembled any type of camp or a white car in the brush. He knew that they could have overlooked anything from flying too high and too low at times. He hopped out of the plane and ran to his car. He had no choice but to find them by foot. They had to be close to another mine.

Bob didn't know the Colombian bosses called Bear and Horse earlier that morning, all hopping mad! Their prisoners used a code between themselves to talk; therefore depriving them what they could learn from them. Interpreters told them they understood only code.

Not knowing what to do, they called Bear and gave him specific instructions to move out of the area immediately. He could make one last sweep of the city of Cagney in search of the one called Bob. If the father of Lucy, Bob's only love, wasn't at home, find him and kill him. They had rather have Bob captured but if it were not possible, they could simply shoot him on sight. The others' strength or durability could be tested by finding out how long they could live under torture.

Bear understood. He called his band together and ordered them to search every building in Cagney except private homes. They would look in theaters and stores of all types. If they caught a hint of Bob living in a private residence, kill or capture him and kill everyone inside.

Their first clue happened in the pool hall. The one who liked to talk and challenge strangers to a game caught the mercenaries' attention. He called himself Hook. They needed to learn about Hook, the man who loved to talk. Bear invited Hook to ride with them. Hook refused. Bear insisted.

Witnesses later told the sheriff that Hook left with them against his will and never returned.

Bob continued to search and finally found a new road with fresh tracks leading to a campsite. He looked carefully through the wide area in search of fresh dirt on the surface that would be the approximate size of bodies buried. That would be where he expected to find his two partners.

With a large, flat stone, he began digging and scrapping out fresh dirt. Minutes later he found the remains of two bearded men that caused him to walk back to his car with a handkerchief covering his nose. He found the chief deputy at his office in Cagney.

Bob accompanied the chief and two deputies to the burial site of which they recognized the local Justice of Peace with his best hunting buddy, owner of Cagney's only liquor store. Both men had been reported missing. The buried men still had their rifles under the dirt, placed comfortably alongside each of their bodies. The sheriff called the F.B.I.

CHAPTER 11

Bob left the city as soon as he found his car and drove to Canada. He picked up Lucy and broke the news of her mother. He then begged her forgiveness for all his inadequacies during her absence.

She couldn't help but blame Bob for her mother's death. She knew that she should have never trusted him. Hours later, her attitude began to silently change. She remained saddened the full duration of the trip and refused to eat. Her young daughter ate twice. Once inside the city limits, he pulled over in the parking lot of the Sheriff's Office.

Exhausted from the lack of sleep, he really didn't know where to begin so he simply began talking. "This isn't the surprise visit I had hoped for, Lucy. I actually believed that I could keep your mother alive."

She began weeping with her back to him but he continued. "If the bad guys are still in town you, your daughter and your dad are in great danger. I have this gut feeling that they have left town. Lucy, I want you to please listen to the sheriff and allow the F.B.I. to help you. They will want to talk with me but that isn't going to happen. All you need to know is that I have not told you one lie since we met a few days ago."

"What are you going to do now?" she asked.

"Do you still have the money I gave you?"

"Yes. I have all of it. Why, do you want it back?" Her voice seemed weak.

"No. Do something with it, all you can for your daughter and yourself."

"Are you leaving right now?"

"Yes. I was hoping you would leave with me."

She scoffed. "You're not even going to stay for my mother's funeral? Even after you indirectly caused her death?"

"I'm sorry that I didn't protect her. I know you don't believe me, but I have told you in the best way I know."

She remained silent a moment until she felt sure of her decision. "Dennis, I don't even know if I ever want to see you again."

He nodded and swallowed his pain. "Take your daughter and things with you to some city like Richmond and never look back. Talk with the sheriff immediately and ask for protection. They'll know when things are safe again."

"I'll do it, Dennis. Why are you too scared to talk with the FBI?"

"I'm not scared, Lucy. It simply would be best if I didn't. You don't know where I'm going and that's for the best. I will call you in a few weeks."

"You really don't need to bother calling me, Dennis."

He sighed heavily while attempting to hide his hurt. "Yes, for my sake, I really do. If you haven't changed your mind by that time, you won't hear from me again. But I've wanted to tell you this a long time, so I'll say it now, since I may not have the chance later. I am in love with you, Lucy. I have always loved you since we dated in our senior year. Each time we saw each other since that time have confirmed my feelings for you."

"Dennis, I can remember your dark wavy hair in high school. I can see that you still have those sharp blue eyes that I was so crazy about. Time and distance, Dennis, have a way of healing things. What I see in you now is that you are obsessed. Grow up and get over it!"

"Lucy, you once promised yourself to me. I had to leave the country. While I was gone, you married this Lewis character who won't even take care of you. Who is it that's obsessed, Lucy?"

"You will forget me in a little while, Dennis."

He controlled his emotions better with a grin. "I kind of doubt it."

She opened the door without looking at him. He spoke her name. She ignored him and carried her things and daughter inside the Sheriff's Office. It was twilight and he wished he could have convinced her to leave with him. He sighed and attempted to face what she said to him. Sickened, he made a U-turn and left.

Bear looked back and noticed Cody making a mess on the floor of the cab. Blood drained from his mouth, mixed with saliva that came with intense pain. "Hey—you--cowboy! Are you uncomfortable or something? Look at that mess you're making!"

Cody's mouth pained him more than he could imagine. He couldn't stop drooling on the floor. Each heartbeat caused a throbbing in every bone in his head. He wished for the aspirin Leo had joked about. When he heard his captor make his taunting remark, his head pained him even more. He wanted to faint or die, anything to rid himself of the pain. He gathered sufficient energy to speak.

"Sorry about that, chief. I think I have a toothache. A box of aspirin would be nice."

"I'll get a pack of napkins. You clean that mess off the floor and spit in a napkin from now on."

Cody knew he would have to tolerate the pain but it seemed to ease as he began to think. He fought the nausea and feared throwing up, which could cause almost any type of infection. "Sounds reasonable, boss. Where are we?"

Bear took a fast look outside and then at his map. "Would you believe North Carolina? We're somewhere inside the state. You and your partner are heavy sleepers."

Cody began to try to make sense with their situation. "I am assuming we are on the move for some reason or other."

Bear agreed. "The boss got upset at the code you used last night. It made no sense. We're supposed to look into it. You want to tell us what's going on with that garble?"

"Leo and I decided to entertain ourselves with a little mixed up Italian that made no sense. It's our own brand of humor between us. No one else is supposed to make sense of it. We sure don't."

Bear grinned. "I hope that you're telling the truth about that. It got us moved out of there *pronto!* Now we got to find a new place in the woods or an empty building somewhere."

Cody tried to peer outside but his chains held him down against the seat. "Well, take your time. You didn't find our buddy, did you?"

"No. We'll find him sooner or later. He'll get careless, just like you guys did."

Cody assured him that they will never find him. "Not to worry, pal. Bob will find you."

Bear pretended not to hear. "Pull in to that little store. I'll get the napkins to clean up that mess he's made. "Are you guys hungry back there?"

"No." Leo answered first. "Oh—I'm hungry but I don't want anything to eat while I'm still holding my head together. My brains will fall out if I let go."

"How about yourself, cowboy? Could you stand some grub? You guys need to keep your strength up. If you think you're in pain now, you're really in for a treat tomorrow or the next day. Neither one of you have a clue in knowing what real pain is like."

"Do you know what real pain is like, bad guy?" Leo asked.

"Not really," Bear answered. "I've watched a few guys sit still while they grimaced from torn nails and toes removed from their feet. I was quite impressed by a few of them that didn't scream their lungs out. After a few hours of honest misery and a few burns over the bodies from a welding torch, they just fell over and died. I guess their hearts quit on them. Who knows?"

"I'll make you and Horse a deal, Bear." Leo said. "You let us go right now, and I'll give you my word that I won't kill you or any of your sick buddies, kinfolks, or whatever else you have."

Bear laughed. "Now that just ain't gonna happen. But keep it up, I'm going to enjoy hearing you beg me to kill you. You'll cry and scream, old buddy."

Leo scoffed. "In your dreams, *old buddy*!"

Bear chuckled again. "Are you hearing this, Mr. Cody?"

Cody said weakly. "If I were you, Bear, I'd listen to him. He's usually not this generous."

Bob knew nothing else. He stood at the end of his trail feeling a total loss. He called Dan and reported finding what he thought was the holding place of Leo and Cody, not even an inkling in where to go from there."

Dan thought carefully before responding. "You might check with the F.B.I., Bob, if you're desperate enough."

"If would mean the end of us, Dan. They would arrest me for taking Lucy out of the country. I'm going to have to rely on gut feelings if you don't have a suggestion."

"I'm sorry, Bob. I have nothing. Keep in touch."

"Yeah," Bob said, feeling further drained. He secured the telephone and felt a strong feeling to tell it goodbye.

He walked to the rental and drove to the next town. There, he pulled over and rested his eyes. Moments later, he heard the word as if he spoke it. "*Tucson.*"

He purchased a road map and studied it. He didn't want to drive there but it made more sense than looking for them in Canada. Of course they could bury his partners or dump them anywhere in a hundred rivers or lakes. He needed help.

In Memphis, he drove to the main office of the FBI. They would have a profiler on hand, somewhere. He dropped the idea. He decided on a shaman or anyone who claimed to be a physic.

Bob knew that terrorists are natural cowards. Like many rational people, they drew strength from their own kind or with people with the same goals. He knew they would dispose of the bodies where the least chance of exposure existed. His face suddenly brightened. "Of course! I'll retrace my steps. Good thinking, Bob!"

"So!" He continued aloud. "Psychics lived everywhere, where do I go to find one?"

CHAPTER 12

Somewhere within North Carolina they moved under the cover of darkness to a motel room. Their guards also showed signs of exhaustion. One guard stayed with them. Both Cody and Leo knew their only chance of escape would be in this place. In the moments required to reach their room, no chance of escape arrived. They looked at one another and Cody's eyes fixed on the telephone inside their room. Leo understood and rose to his feet. One guard couldn't watch both of them.

"I need to use the bathroom." Cody said weakly.

The guard, who spoke decent English, expressed the same thing. He pointed to Leo and said, "You wait!"

Leo protested. Cody followed the guard into the bathroom. The guard pushed Cody back. Cody insisted slightly, not enough to rouse anyone else and to let the guard know that he could be manhandled by one man, alone. He almost fell back.

The guard scoffed and disappeared behind the door. Cody followed. They began to scuffle. Leo wasted no time. He lifted the hook and dialed Dan's number in Bogota. He didn't want to talk, he simply wanted to dial the number and hear it ring until the answering machine took over.

The guard used some language in Spanish that Leo failed to recognize. Cody fell to the floor the blaring instant the guard hit him in the mouth. He groaned loudly and slammed his hands against his lower body as if in great pain. Leo stood with his back to the telephone and listened for connections. The process seemed extremely slow. He pretended to move toward the door. The guard met him and pointed his finger, advising him silently, to leave well enough alone.

Leo tested him and got struck in the face. He feigned pain and staggered backward. The guard felt well pleased with himself. The two Americans didn't seem so tough.

Cody still moved and kept the man's attention. Leo faced him with his back hiding the telephone. Cody made a noise in great pain. Leo finally heard words on the telephone and hoped it wasn't the motel clerk. He dropped the receiver back into its cradle. The guard rushed around him to only see the telephone in place.

Cody raised himself from the floor slowly. He paid no attention to Leo as he dropped on the bed. The guard returned to the bathroom and finished his business. Everything to him appeared normal. He finally helped Cody to the bathroom and watched Leo, who returned his venomous stare.

Alone in his office early the following morning, Dan checked the fax first then the telephone's answering machine. He found one call on the device without a voice. He called the operator and persuaded her to search for the number, she called back several times telling him it was impossible. He told her that everyone would be well paid. She tried a moment longer. Even though it could be nothing, Dan hoped for the best. The operator kept calling him back protesting against the impossible task. He kept telling them that everyone would be paid.

He then sat and wondered at the extreme likelihood that it might well be a wrong number, but he knew his men and if Cody or Leo didn't want to talk, the tape would be blank.

His office secretaries came in and fixed coffee. They both asked him to go after some sweet bread. He then had to deal with the two of them as well as the operators. After more than an hour, the local operator called Dan and told him their time would be on his bill. He asked for the trace's results. The call originated from a motel in Martinville, North Carolina. The U. S. operators traced it for free for the operators in Bogota.

Dan didn't know if he wasted time or not. It seemed logical for Leo or Cody to still be alive. On the other hand, such a call from a motel in North Carolina seemed more of a mistake than anything else. He shifted his attention to his office. Both his secretaries still pouted and refused to talk with him unless he produced the sweet bread. He found something akin to doughnuts a few blocks away. Chocolate fudge covered them. He cringed at the thought of eating one but his secretaries made a fuss over them.

Bob asked the homicide detective at the nearest police station if he had ever used a psychic. The detective didn't believe in them but admitted that the entire team used one about a year prior.

"Was he any good?" Bob asked. "I have a cold case going. I'm not a cop but I do want to find my friends who disappeared a few days ago."

"Here's her address and telephone number," the detective said as if he could be no further help to Bob. "Good luck with the voo doo stuff."

Bob called the number and got her husband, who said she had a bad cold. Bob explained that he was in desperate need of help. He waited several minutes, hearing a lady protest in the background. No doubt about the bad cold. He heard her coughing and sneezing.

"Can I help you, sir?" she finally asked.

Bob explained that his friends were kidnapped by bad guys in Cagney, W. Virginia a few days ago. She listened and asked him the ages of his two friends and if they were married. He told her about both men, what they liked and disliked. He admitted to killing several drug dealers in a foreign country, all in self-defense. She asked him to wait while she attempted to sort out the many new pictures and conflicting happenings in her head, some of them in color.

He waited patiently several minutes before she talked again. "Hello, sir?"

"Yes, Ma'am!" he answered hurriedly.

"Drive to my house and give my husband two twenties. He will tell you what I have learned."

Bob hurried to the address and stopped by a yard gate and a mailbox. A man stood waiting by the mailbox. Bob pulled alongside the man and held out the twenties.

After taking them and placing them securely in his shirt pocket, he said. "This ain't much but she had a lot of information going inside her head all at the same time. She said that the married man's wife was extremely worried and that she lived out south or west in a large city, maybe even as far south as California. She also said that several men traveled to the south and west. Some of them were hurt bad. She believes the husband is in that group. It is very confusing to her with that bad cold."

Bob thanked the man and left. "Better than nothing," he said aloud. He didn't expect to hang around Memphis any longer than to what he had accomplished. They seem to be traveling southwest he thought. That's where he wanted them to travel and that's where he headed in his rental.

He stopped and called Dan, who told him that he received a call from someone who left no message from a motel in Martinsville, North Carolina.

Bob said, "Our men may be in Canada or Mongolia, Dan, but I'm headed for the Carolina woods as we speak."

"The best of luck to you, Bob!"

"Yeah," Bob said, "the best of luck to us both."

Bob stopped at the first telephone booth and called the psychic lady again in Memphis. This time, she answered.

"Did you give the money to my husband?" she asked.

"Yes, ma'am, I gave him two twenties like you asked. He put them in his right shirt pocket and buttoned it. Have you had anymore revelations on the men traveling westward?"

"I recall that I saw a shiny white truck in the midst of it all. It's a large one with big wheels and a big cab, but I couldn't see anything else because darkness surrounded the truck and many men who had no faces or colored clothes. They were all in darkness. The truck was definitely white."

"Do you think they were traveling west?" he asked.

"No. Now that I'm thinking about it, I am getting a southward feeling. It's strong!"

Bob headed for North Carolina.

Bear called his contact in Bogota. "I don't feel right here in this crowded state." He said. "I'd like to dump the both of them on a dirt road somewhere if I could fine one without a shiny black pickup parked on it."

The contact said to be patient and return to Cagney. The town is full of FBI, so get rid of your truck and buy a van. I want that woman and her dad finished more than killing those two you have with you. Take your time. With the woman and her father dead, the one called Bob will make a showing. You shouldn't have left in the first place!"

Bear, disgusted, said, "Yes, you're probably right but I was following your orders."

Bob drove south an hour before stopping and calling the psychic again. "Ma'am, I'm sorry for pressuring you. I'll pay for the information if you could help me a bit more."

She breathed in deeply and coughed before saying anything. "Things have slowed down since you left. This time, ring the door bell and give me the two twenties. My husband won't return before the money you gave him is gone."

"I'll be there in an hour or two." He said, feeling new hope building inside. "Ma'am, is there anything I can bring you for that cold?"

She told him that she would appreciate a bottle of aspirin and nose drops. He could also bring two lemons and a small bottle of whiskey. "You can take the price of these things out of the two twenties that I want for the information. I'm sorry to have to charge you for a talent that God gave me, but I need medication. My husband is a drunk. He won't last much longer before he drowns in the creek near here."

Bob had already made his U-turn and felt like the lady was more legitimate than he had hoped. He drove to the outskirts of Memphis again and stopped at a store that sold gas.

Two hours total passed before he stopped in front of the house again. He rang the doorbell with the hand holding the two twenties.

She didn't look at the money but the sack he held. "Come in," she said. "You won't catch my cold if you keep your distance. You can put the stuff and money on the kitchen table and sit there while I talk."

He sat on the couch in the living room. She seemed tidy, fortyish, and would be a handsome woman with makeup and her hair untangled. She wore a thin slip under her open house robe.

"I'm sorry for my appearance," she said. "You seem like an okay fella. Now, I want you to start all over again and tell me from the beginning. I'm pretty sure I have you mixed up with Mrs. Morgan's problems but a lot of things have fallen on me and covered me all up completely. Some of it is beginning to make sense. She touched the sack that he placed on the table and stood still before turning back to him.

"You have a girl in Cagney, don't you?"

"Lucy," he said. "I'm not so sure we are ever going to be together."

She agreed, which caused his heart to grow heavier. "Tell me everything!" She said and sat down hurriedly in the kitchen chair. "Lucy is what I was missing. I was getting Laverne out of this mess. Go ahead, talk to me."

He did, completely believing in her. He began with his brother telling his friends that he was in Cagney. He told her the names of his friends and the states where they were raised. Anything else about them could increase the danger. He told her about taking Lucy to Canada.

She listened and nodded. Occasionally, she muttered the word, "Yes."

CHAPTER 13

"Mr. Bob," she began. "The men you have chasing you are bad men. Very bad! I don't just say this because they murdered your friend, Mrs. Moore. I say it in addition to that fact from the sights and thoughts I've had. I actually thought the murdered woman was a close friend of Mrs. Morgan, who lives here in this city. Her problems and yours have become intermingled."

"My story to you, ma'am, is true," he stated solemnly. "But hardly anyone believes me. I have nowhere to go without my two friends. I've got to get them back."

"As of this moment, your friends are either back in Cagney or they are going there. They are alive but very ill. I believe they are at the hands of many, bad men. I cannot tell you how much longer they will live. I do feel like they are alive. I don't know for sure, of course."

Bob stood up. "Ma'am, if they are back in Cagney, they will kill Lucy as soon as she's identified. I have to leave here now!"

"Yes, go!" the strange woman urged. "Try and save your loved one and keep her alive. The same goes for your friends. I wish you well, sir!"

He was on his way to the door when she stopped him. "Mr. Bob, I just visualized a car wreck. Drive carefully!"

"Always, ma'am. I am never careless with an automobile."

"I'm not saying it was you involved. I just visualized a car speeding on a highway in the woods and crashing. Those types of vehicle accidents are hard to avoid."

He agreed with her. "Was this at night?"

"I don't know."

Bob would be parking his car for hours if necessary. But he couldn't afford the time anymore that he could afford an accident. He knew that no one predicts the future, but he believed the psychic.

She added: "My predictions may have already happened, Mr. Bob. Something else to consider is the fact that I'm not always right."

"Ma'am" he asked. "Are you a Christian?"

"I try to be. My pastor wants me to see an exorcist. He says that God doesn't pass out this type of talent to people. Well, I know that He does because I have it! The good Lord also knows that I don't want it. I would have myself exorcized if I thought for one second that it came from Satan, but it don't. And believe me, sir, uh, Mr. Bob, as much as I like helping people, I have to charge them money. I cannot focus on any type of work if I'm hit with the pictures and stories. I just want everyone to know that I don't like taking their money but I have to live."

"Yes, ma'am, I believe you. I was told when I was a kid that I had an aunt that could do these things. She didn't like it, either."

Cody awoke from a nap mixed with waking nightmare of pain. "Hey, boss! Are we there yet?"

"No. We have a few hours to go yet. We won't be stopping until we arrive."

"I dislike being nosey, sir, but where are we going?"

"We're headed back to Cagney, cowboy! Our boss decided we had to finish our job there."

Cody's mouth suddenly felt worse. "Are we going to be tortured and buried in the woods again?"

"Just as soon as we can set up the cameras and sound equipment, old buddy! That radio is something else. It cost many thousands of dollars to reach all the way to Colombia, but the closer we are to the ocean, the better the frequencies travel. The tallest tree makes the best antenna."

"Fantastic!" Leo almost shouted. "Your boss might have just signed your death warrants."

"Sure!" Bear said, almost laughing. "Our group takes nothing for granted and we're always careful."

"Yeah?" Leo was relentless. "You guys have thus far ambushed two unsuspecting hunters and murdered a defenseless old lady. Your test is coming when one man will wipe you off the face of this earth as easily as ordering ham and eggs for breakfast."

Bear laughed for real this time. "We've been tested before by some pretty tough warriors. We're still here to pop a few caps into your bodies and bury you while you're practically insane from pain."

Cody said, "Let's not talk about pain anymore. My mouth is already hurting enough!"

Leo said to Cody, "You'd better put a sock in it, crybaby, if you want to make probation."

Cody replied in Italian: "I quit!"

Bear said, "Here, now! It's rude to spout a foreign language when you're in the presence of people who don't understand. But if I'm not mistaken, cowboy, you just told your buddy to take this job and shove it?"

"In so many words," Cody said. "I just resigned."

"Who are you guys working for?"

"His name is Bob," Leo answered. "We work for him as private investigators."

Bear believed him. "That's what Alfred Luminato told us. But I find it hard to believe that a couple or three private investigators would tackle an army of security forces in South America. Did you get paid well?"

Leo spoke up. "We did it for free. I don't accept pay to have fun."

"Wow!" Bear said and whistled. "Private investigators that work for free! You'll have to excuse my skepticism!"

Leo said, "Ah-you're too young and inexperienced to understand what goes on in the real world, Bear."

Horse spoke up. "Boss, let's stop and cut some fingers and toes off these two smart mouths."

Cody said, "I have already closed my mouth!"

"Ditto!" Leo followed rapidly.

The F.B.I. agent set up his new headquarters in the sheriff's private office. His district supervisor recommended that one agent answer the sheriff's call for help. However, a second agent from another city joined the first hours later. Both men recommended that Lucy, her daughter and her father be locked in cells until more suitable quarters could be found. The agents also postponed Mrs. Moore's funeral to an uncertain date.

By daylight the following morning all residents and the mine's employees in the mining town of Cagney knew that the remaining Moore family had been jailed by the F.B.I. The majority of them thought Tommy Moore cheated on his taxes.

The agents asked the sheriff to call his entire force of deputies for a meeting. The sheriff sat next to an agent at a table facing the deputies. No city police or constables existed in Cagney, since the mining community never rated a city status. The lead agent spoke after the sheriff introduced him.

"According to information from a man we call Bob an uncertain number of mercenaries are here to kill Lucy Mullins, her child, and her parents. Thus far, this woman's mother has, indeed, been murdered in her home. The reason for this incredible strategy is that certain drug cartels in Colombia want to kill the loved ones of Bob. That part is standard with the employees of all cartels in Colombia. The word is that Bob, along with two other men played havoc in a couple families near Bogota. This same Bob has been in love with Lucy Moore Mullins since high school, but she, apparently, did not have the same feelings for Bob as she married a local man. He has since left her here with her parents. Bob, whom the Moores refer, is Dennis Ferguson who hails from Memphis. The remaining of the Moore family is held for safe keeping only and no one has cheated on his taxes. That is the story as we have it thus far. Bob, it seems, is nowhere around.

"Now the reason we don't have a warrant for Bob's arrest is that the sheriff found the gravesite of two innocent victims who stumbled upon the crude site where Bob's two associates were supposedly captured. It is the gravesites for Judge Holcomb and his hunting partner for years, the local liquor store owner and operator. The possibility that Bob murdered the two hunters and buried them just to throw suspicion away from himself has not been ruled out.

"Bob came to Cagney with the story that mercenaries hired by some drug cartels were out to kill the three men who killed many of their employees and brought destruction upon the headquarters of one strong drug cartel. A Tucson attorney bought the remainder of this property and turned it back into a major cocaine plantation. Unfortunately, this owner was murdered by Bob and his two friends.

"The day Bob came to Cagney, he practically kidnapped Lucy Mullens and her daughter from the Moore residence. He invited Mrs. Moore along, who refused. Bob carried Lucy and her daughter to a shelter for battered women in Canada. After Mrs. Moore had been murdered by the so-called mercenaries, Bob retrieved Lucy and her child from the safe house in Canada and brought her home. He left Cagney immediately. This man is to be detained for further questioning. Look for him in this area. We will obtain a nationwide murder warrant on him in the near future.

"While these three men may be hailed as national heroes, they are presently the FBI's most wanted. Since they cannot be traced to any legal agency in this country, we assume they are vigilantes working for someone very rich who wishes to remain anonymous. We do not know their names or with whom they may be associated. Some say they are free lancers working for Bob, who owns a private detective agency somewhere in the United States. We cannot locate his agency.

"Therefore, any and all strangers in this city are to be detained for questioning. The entire force will be working 12-hour shifts around the clock until we think the suspects have been located or until further notice."

The sheriff spoke up. "I know this Bob as Bob, nothing else. I took him as an intelligent man who moved quietly and took his time to formulate his thoughts before speaking. He is likeable, convincing, and very confident. If he is a killer, and I doubt if he is, be both cautious and courteous upon detaining him.

"Now the question I have for the FBI is this: We need manpower. When do we get it?"

CHAPTER 14

The leading FBI agent cleared his voice. "Until we gain further knowledge of the actual threat of mercenaries, you will work in pairs, or if you deem it necessary, work four men to a car. Then, based on necessity, there will be no limit to your manpower. I'm sorry, but for the present, that's all I can do."

The sheriff stood up. "We have three vehicles, counting mine. Use your two and work in pairs. If any of you need to go home to refresh your extended time on duty, feel free to do so. Alvin has prepared a schedule which includes him working with a different partner until this mess blows over. Be safe!"

Bob drove all night. He did stop earlier at sundown and waited an hour before continuing. He saw no vehicular accidents on the way. Once he arrived in Cagney, he stopped at the city limits and backed his rental into the trees off the main highway.

He released the catch on his backrest and let it down. He still heard road noises and felt a light dizziness settle over him. An overcast caused the trees surrounding him seem greener and darker, giving off a strong scent of pines that he loved. He drifted into sleep and thought he heard rain spattering the roof.

He slept two hours. The driver's side window remained open he felt unlimited waves of coolness pass through the comforts of his vehicle and refreshed the entire forest. He could hear any sound from the highway and promised himself to wake if a vehicle passed his location.

A vehicle did pass while he slept soundly. He thought he heard the short sound of a siren but it blended with other thoughts in a dream where a busy street in a city dominated all thoughts and sounds. He moved through that unknown street without making any sense of his actions or why it existed. A more comfortable thought caught his attention so he mounted the cushion of air and found himself resting in the backseat of a twin-engine airplane. It purred softly until it banked suddenly. With Cody at the controls, always fearless, unsettled versions of crashes stopped all stability in his dream. Fear gripped him as they skimmed the treetops of a heavy forest!

He gasped and snapped awake.

"Cody!" He grumbled audibly. "What are you doing in my personal dreams?"

Bob stepped out and walked around his vehicle in order to wake himself. "Too long without a restful sleep," he muttered and held his forehead a second and became fully awake, "You and Leo are captured together! Oh—Lord!"

He drove toward Cagney, almost speeding. He drove passed the sheriff's office where the jail cells made up a large portion of the building. Cars moved quietly and the parked cars enjoyed the overcast instead of a hot sun cooking them on the heated asphalt. He shook his head, "Bob," he ordered himself, "go back to bed and wake up before you stumble blindly into trouble."

He found his small patch of trees that crowded together more than the larger trees spaced apart. He wished he had purchased a sandwich in town but he really didn't need it due to sitting so long in a car without exercise. In no time, he drifted back to sleep.

Later the following afternoon, a van rolled passed Bob's position and eased further into town observing all traffic laws. Cody lay on the middle seat of the van, attempting to sleep on chains that held him tight to the seat. He thought he felt the van slowing for a turn but didn't care. Leo lay quietly on the back seat.

The van stopped. He heard Bear's fiendish voice. "Okay, Horse. Make sure the guys in the pickup are at their best. Lock and load. We're going to do a number on that hillbilly jail house. Just kill any and everybody in and out of the cells. That will take care of the Moore family in order for Bob to know. Then we start on these two in the back."

Cody attempted to straighten up. "Bear! If you have any decency left in your body, don't do this! Those people are innocent!"

Bear grinned and said, "Cody, old friend, what we are about to do will be clean, fast and merciful, nothing like what we're going to do to you. Show some appreciation. Please!"

Cody lay helpless while Bear and his crew left without saying another word. He listened for a lifetime of silence then heard what he dreaded most. Two fast shots jarred his sore mouth open. Seconds later he heard two more shots. A man yelled. He thought it might be Horse's voice but realized it was only wishful thinking.

Two more rapid shots sounded and followed by another interval of chilling silence. A discharge from a shotgun blasted through the broken silence. Another blast followed. He wished he could be there to help the unsuspecting jailer and dispatcher.

Bob awoke from a deep sleep in the nearby woods. He didn't realize that he could be so tired. He had slept for hours. He drove straight to the jail. On his way a pair of red lights came on behind him. The mounted lights above the windshield of a luxury sedan caught his attention. Bob pulled over fast and braked safely for the car behind him that seemed to ride on his back bumper, which he deemed ridiculous.

A call from behind reached him from the sedan's loud speaker. "Driver, exit the vehicle facing in the opposite direction of my voice. That's right! Walk backwards toward me without turning. Two guns are on your back. If you turn or do anything without being told, we will shoot you without delay. That's it, friend. Walk slowly. There, now lie down on your belly! You don't need to know who we are, but since we haven't told you, we are the county deputies covering the city of Cagney, West Virginia."

Bob said, "Very good! I know who you are. I am armed with a nine mil auto under my belt buckle. My name is Bob."

"Very good, Bob! We heard about you from the sheriff. But the F.B.I. knows you as a mysterious private eye that may be a vigilante. They even think that you may have killed Mrs. Moore, conspiracy-wise. No need of lying face down, now. We ain't going to cuff you and you sure ain't under arrest. The F.B.I. doesn't like you, so that makes you one of the good guys in my book. However, since you are a mysterious sort, consider yourself detained with prejudice."

"Prejudice?" Bob asked. "What's that to do with detainment?"

"I don't know," the deputy admitted with a certain amount of embarrassment. The F.B.I. agent suggested that we use it."

Bob slowly stood up and shook both their hands. "If I'm not mistaken, the same F.B.I. agent wants to put me behind bars more than anything else. His suspicions are no more than his lack of confidence. Believe me on that."

"That he is, Mr. Bob. "You might add a little emphasis on wanting you behind bars."

Bob straightened his clothes and said, "I'm glad we have the bureau. They were a useful force in the J. Edgar days."

They both grinned and waited for him to talk more.

"Okay, guys, let me tell you what we're up against. Mercenaries. These people are not particular about who they kill because they like it. Sometimes their work is simply terrorism. They consider themselves fortunate to be paid to kill, which is what it's all about. They like it. It's their favorite way of applying terrorism. However, they are not the cowards that terrorists are. They will fight, cornered or not. They have the skill and guts to face their opponents because they are well trained and they will strike without warning. They have no sense of fair play in any situation. In other words, they act outside the law and you act within it. That gives them the advantage."

"Sounds like they may be kind of dishonest." the driver said, grinning.

The police radio from the sedan sputtered words and static. "Officers down at the S.O! Officers down!"

"That's them!" Bob shouted at their backs. "Shoot on sight. Do not hesitate! Hesitation gives them an advantage!"

Bob tried to keep up with the cruiser but fell far behind. A moment later the cruiser braked and skidded sideways half a city block amid a cloud of smoke from burned rubber and brown dust. The two uniformed officers rushed forward, guns leading their way. Bob looked around and found a new van parked opposite the S.O. building. A new pickup, white, parked closely behind it. Just as Bob found a space, the van came alive and rushed forward, barely missing Bob's left front fender.

Bob braked short of the pickup and spun his steering wheel to do a U-turn behind the van. The van turned on to the road Bob just left and fish-tailed while gaining speed.

Bob floored the rental and fell in behind. Surprisingly, his rental reached ninety-five mph but the van still gained distance on him.

Cody, though jostled and in severe pain, moved inside his chains and handcuffs. Leo also got jostled awake. "What's happening, Bear?"

No answer.

Cody raised himself from his seat as far as possible and saw Horse driving. *This man was in escape mode!* He wondered what transpired moments ago. With Bear gone, his and Leo's lives fell short of surviving a few minutes passed the time this man slowed down. He tried to free one foot and kept trying until they could work together.

He slid on the seat as far as possible and placed both boots on the backrest of Horse's seat. He shoved against the seat as powerful as possible. It gave slightly.

"What tha..."

Cody drew his knees in as far as possible and kicked again. This time the speeding van almost turned over as it went sideways, straightened and skidded headlong into a large tree. Cody and Leo bounced forward until their painful chains stopped them. Horse sat unconscious against the loud horn.

Bob skidded behind the van and stopped equally abruptly. He rushed forward to check the driver.

The driver appeared unconscious. He heard moaning from the back. He opened the door and Cody looked up at him.

Without having seen the man in months, Cody spoke his most important thoughts. "Do you have any aspirin on you, Bob?"

Leo moaned from the back seat. Bob looked passed Cody's seat and found Leo dangling from chains off the rear seat. One chain choked him at his throat. Bob quickly moved that chain.

"Before the driver wakes," Bob borrowed some of Leo's humor, "tell me if you guys are kidnapping this poor man against his wishes."

Leo said, "Bob, you aren't a comedian. It would appear that you might have learned a little from me--but who am I fooling?"

Cody talked as loud as his pain would allow, "Never-mind us! Check that driver! If he's not dead, make him that way without further hesitation!"

Gun still in hand, Bob jerked the driver's door open in time to find a shot-gun barrel come up. Bob shot fast, sending two bullets in the chest from an angle and one in the man's temple.

Blood spurted immediately backward from the head across Cody's feet, who said, "Bob! Why don't you watch what you're doing!"

"Never-mind him, Bob!" Leo yelled. "Get me out of this mess!"

Bob opened the door to where he could see Leo, who hang horizontally from chains around the seat. Bob worked until coming to a lock. He looked at Cody and said, "I hope this driver has a key. I smell gas."

Bob unfastened the seatbelt and yanked the dead man out to a prone position in the tall weeds. He found keys in the front pocket.

Once freed and sitting on the ground near Bob's car, they looked up to see a cruiser brake and stop short of the van. The sheriff stepped out and approached Bob. "Are you okay, Mr. Bob?"

"Yeah! I found my two partners, too. They were locked in the seats in the van."

"What happened at the station, Sheriff? I heard the call on the cruiser."

The Sheriff looked at Cody and Leo. Cody had blood smeared across his face. Both men needed a shave. "Well, things came down pretty fast. Both agents of the esteemed F.B.I. were there. One bought it when two men suddenly came busting through the door. The other agent rolled and fired back at the same time but he hit no one. He hid behind the door leading to the cells. The dispatcher near the front door was shot. He died immediately after I arrived."

Cody said, "We were both lying on the back seats chained. I heard shots. I shoved the driver up against the steering wheel and we crashed. Bob shot him before he shot us. The only name we know from him is Horse. He and the boss called Bear were going to kill us in front of cameras and audio equipment so the people in Bogota could watch and hear our death cries."

The sheriff grunted. "He may be one of the two that busted through the door and killed the agent. If he is, the other one got away."

"There were four men." Leo said. "The one that got away sounds like it may be the leader called Bear."

"Okay, the F.B.I. will want to hear all this from you guys." The sheriff said.

Bob held up his hand. "All in due time, sir. Right now we have our own schedule. I have made my report to you. The F.B.I. is secondary and not the primary law enforcement in this area. They can wait for us until we secure Bear in the dead mode or behind bars."

The sheriff made a passing motion with his hand. "I don't know who any of you guys are or nothing about you. I'm leaving it for the F.B.I. to sort it out."

Cody said, "If I'm not mistaken, Bear, at this very moment is on the telephone with a Bogota cartel leader asking for a new crew and one much larger. The Colombians won't allow this to this to blow over until several Americans die. They want the three of us, our families, friends, and they won't quit until we're all dead."

"Well, that's too bad for you guys. If you hang around here, you will be talking to the F.B.I., like it or not. I have no choice but to support the F.B.I."

Bob understood. Cody told the sheriff that they were no one important and that they need to leave immediately without wasting valuable time with the F.B.I.

"Okay, I believe that you are either scared of the F.B.I. or else you're wanted."

Bob said, "We aren't wanted, Sheriff. What we do and who we work for is highly confidential, very secret. We are good guys."

The sheriff continued. "Here's what the agent saw, according to him. Two men came through the door, each one shot. One bullet struck his partner in the head and the other passed over the head of the other agent. He said he fired back at the two men but they both dived between some desks. He saved his bullets. Then two more men burst in fast. They were both Hispanic and firing fast. The agent shot both of them while they fired at him. He was immediately out of ammo but he won the firefight. The two white men escaped. Me? I saw one vehicle leave and I went after it. I'm glad it was you guys."

Bob nodded and said, "I think we have the picture of what happened. These two guys and I are going to disappear. We're hoping to cut the head off the monster before new mercenaries are hired. You may not see us again. But before we go, please allow me to show you how to fight mercenaries. The F.B.I. will not teach you. Law enforcement must stay inside guide lines. Guide lines with mercenaries will get you killed."

"Save it!" the sheriff said. "I wasn't born inside a coal mine. I read and watch all the television I need."

CHAPTER 15

Bear ran passed the van and pickup parked on the street. He preferred to remain on foot instead of taking a chance on being chased by vehicles. He knew that houses would provide a temporary cover. He sprinted across a vacant lot and kept putting distance between him and the main highway. Still running at top speed, he passed three residences and stopped at the first one with an open door. He rushed inside looking to the sides carefully without a thought of who might be there. It didn't matter so long as he held the gun.

A middle-aged woman closed the door to her bathroom and walked through the kitchen, keeping her eyes on the man that barged into her home. "Who are you?" she demanded.

Bear stood up and bowed slightly. "I am terribly sorry, madam! But there has been a shooting at the sheriff's office a few blocks away and I was only standing by long enough to get myself out of there!"

"Well, what're you doin' in my house?"

"I'm sorry, madam! I barged in under emergency conditions. I need to use your telephone."

"You can't be making any long distance calls on my telephone!"

Bear pulled his gun and walked to her. "Shut your mouth, you old hen, or I'll blow it out of your head! Turn around!"

She began crying and squirming while she turned and Bear swung at the back of her head with all his strength. He heard her skull crack. She fell while crying out only once. Without hesitating or considering compassion for a helpless woman, he dropped to his knees, grabbed her chin and quickly twisted her neck until it snapped.

No longer considering her a nuisance, he snatched the telephone and began dialing, feeling far more relaxed. Once he reached a Bogota operator, he asked for his boss's ranch.

It required more time than Bear liked, the lawyer who spoke English finally came to the telephone. "This is Tomas. To whom am I speaking?"

This man controlled Bear and his crew. He spoke with intelligence, firmness and all the conviction needed to impress and motivate his hired killers. Bear liked all men who knew how to lead naturally. In the military, this man would be a colonel. He quickly brought the chief up to date.

"I need help here, boss. These hillbilly deputies are ducks in a barrel, but the men you want dead are slick and move like monkeys in trees. Horse panicked and ran off with them. If he don't kill them fast, they'll kill him. Horse is a hard case, anyhow, Tomas. He needs replacing. He likes to maim and kill then move on to another victim. I need an assistant who can think objectively."

"Then find him, Bear! I don't have the time and patience for you people to choose your favorite type of grunt!"

Bear grinned. "I know just the man in Chicago, but you're gonna have to come up with some big bucks. He's as expensive as I am."

Tomas said, "Stop wasting my time and do your job! We have all the money you need!"

Bear slammed the telephone down and ran out the back way. This caused dogs to bark so he turned back to the street. A young lady driving a small red car approached from the south. He stepped in front holding one arm high in a friendly gesture.

Bob drew lines on the ground with a stick and pointed out the highways leading into Cagney. "Sheriff, if the F.B.I. tells you any different than this, don't believe 'em. This man that we are after can and will kill you before you can take the time to identify yourself!"

The sheriff grumbled. "That ain't our way. It may be yours, but we work inside the law."

"I wish you the best, sheriff. The men that are apt to come are like terrorists. The difference is that terrorists are most always cowards. Mercenaries are not cowards. They will not surrender to anybody unless the conditions are in their favor. If the F.B.I. disagrees with me, then let them do the arresting."

One deputy said, "I like this man's attitude, boss."

The sheriff grumbled and looked up. "So do I, but we have to be lawful."

Cody spoke up. "Terrorists come totally unexpected. Age, sex and innocence are nothing to them. The more innocents they kill the more we hate them. This is their objective, hate and fear. Mercenaries love it. They come to kill, and kill they will. Innocents, to them, are nothing but collateral damage.

"If your men make traffic stops, hopefully they are known residents. If it's a strange vehicle, like a rental, be cautious. While the driver is pulling over, a gunman will suddenly fill the back window and fire a shotgun or an automatic weapon at you. Watch for strangers filling an automobile or a truck of any kind. Watch for any vehicle you don't know in your county or city with more than one or two people."

A deputy spoke up. "This is pretty much common sense."

Leo leaned over and slapped the ground beside him. "Exactly! Use it in the next days and weeks!"

The sheriff stood up. "Thanks for the safety course that we still don't need, gentlemen. By the way, if you aren't vigilantes, do you mind telling me who you work for?"

Cody said, "We are not vigilantes. We are lawfully employed and lawfully commissioned. We will not tell you who we work for. I'm sorry but that's a promise to our employers."

The sheriff nodded. "I believe you. The F.B.I. will not like it. In fact, it will fill the mainstream news media for a week!"

Bob grimaced. "That hasn't happened, yet. If it does, our jobs are finished. We will be automatically retired. Until we have Bear in custody or dead, leave everything to the F.B.I. Let them do the suicide work."

Leo stood up and pulled Cody up beside him. "Some agents of the F.B.I. are okay."

Bob turned and looked at Leo. "Leo, will you please knock that brown nosing stuff off?"

"Yes, boss, but I want Cody to be in charge. I'm beginning to get uneasy with you, being wishy washy and everything. All this talk of shooting first and asking questions later scares me."

Two deputies looked at one another and grinned. Both knew that the stocky built Irishman loved to dig his friends with his own type of humor.

Bob ignored him.

As soon as the deputies began to load in their cruisers, one called to Bob. "Hey! Just how good are you guys with a shooter?"

Bob turned to answer while Cody and Leo opened the doors of Bob's rental and grinned. "One of these days, deputy, sooner or later, we won't be good enough!"

"The FBI agent in charge showed his anger. He sat behind the Chief Deputy's desk and glared at the men who had disappointed him. "I have lost a man here! I don't know who we are up against and you had this Bob and his crew in your presence and you didn't bring them in for questioning. Why not?"

The Chief Deputy, a much older man, had removed his hat as did the deputies. He reset it atop his head and said, "Get out of my chair! Get from behind my desk! If you don't like the way I run this station, leave!"

"I'm not leaving, Chief. You can have your office back but I'm setting up a center here in town with a full crew. You guys can work with me or stay out of our way. Either way, I want full cooperation, which will include why you let those men out of your sight without questioning."

"You've had your report. That's all you're getting from us. I questioned Bob and his men to suit me. Bob's story turned out correct. I am satisfied, my deputies are satisfied, and we will resume our task of running our end of the county."

The FBI agent stood firm. "How did Bob's story prove correct? What are their plans? Most of all, who are they?"

The chief responded in a firm voice, "They had no identification that we cared to see. They are not vigilantes. They work undercover and incognito for a federal service, probably the Attorney General's Department of Justice; you know, like the F.B.I? Actually, I think they're headed for South America. Something was said about laying some cartels to waste. You're federal. You probably know something about that." The chief continued.

The agent snatched his jacket off the hangar.

"Now, before you leave I have something else to say. This is for the benefit of you and your men moving into our county. I suggest you brief your men on combatting mercenaries, not the common criminal element that you're used to arresting and fighting. They may or may not be coming, but if and when they do, they will want to kill Bob and his two men, along with the three people we have locked up. If you can, please take Lucy Mullins, her daughter, and her father to a federal safe house. If you can't, they will remain in our safe care as long as our building stays in its present condition."

"How do you know these men are from the Department of Justice?"

The chief shrugged his shoulders. "I don't. But I believed them when they stated they were officially commissioned. They are disappearing for a few days to recuperate. They may be back and they may not. My suggestion for you and your troops is to cooperate and try not to bring them in for anything. This is no more than friendly advice, agent. Frankly, I trust them to fight the mercenaries more than I trust you or anyone else to arrest them. They will be successful because they will fight on the mercenary's terms. Are we on the same page, yet?"

The agent turned red-faced. His fists clenched. "In other words, you want us to leave in order that you can turn this area into a war zone. Is that it?"

"Not at all. I think you and your field of agents will lose in your attempts to arrest the bad guys under our constitutional rules of arrest and seizure."

The agent walked to the door. "I'll leave. If you and your deputies lose one citizen in this county, or if you lose private property to guns and big armament, I'll bring you under charges from a list that it will take an hour to read."

The chief deputy smiled and loosened his hat from around his forehead. "I'm not agreeing to that, either. I'm agreeing to is this: We will guard this county building in full force while you lose every man that attempts to arrest a mercenary, whether it's one or a dozen."

The agent nodded. "I beg your pardon, Chief. I'll leave but my promise to you about losing a citizen or property stands."

The chief said, "Goodbye, sir. I am truly sorry for your losing a man to a more prepared force's ambush."

CHAPTER 16

The young lady in the red car braked to a stop on Cagney Street. The man seemed desperate once he held his hands up and stood in front of her car.

She rolled her window down and smiled at the stranger, who suddenly pointed his gun at her face. She gasped and almost pressed the accelerator. Bear quickly used his other hand to jerk the gear lever out of drive and into the park position.

Bear never lost his broad smile. "Slide over, honey. We're going for a ride."

She obeyed but spoke in a pleading voice. "Please, sir. Take my car but leave me! I have two small kids at home!"

"Why aren't they with you?" he asked.

"They're with my little sister, who watches them while I take my husband to work! Please don't hurt me!"

Bear drove with one hand and held the gun pointed at her middle. "Relax, sugar! This isn't about sex or injury. It's about me having a car for my get-away. So settle down and act normal. I'll set you free once we clear town."

She hid her face in the corner of her backrest and the passenger door and cried. "No. You're going to kill me. I know it and so do you!"

Bear's face showed disappointment. "Hey, pretty baby! That's not nice! We're taking a ride. Keep your harsh comments to yourself or we might have a party in the backseat before I set you free. Are we clear?"

She continued to cry. He turned on the main road and drove back through town, passed the Sheriff's Office, and the people gathering around it. His truck still remained parked. But Horse had pulled up stakes. He had to be far down the road in the van by now. Catching up would require speeding, and that would prove unhealthy in this hick town. He drove until he ran out of houses before pulling over.

She stopped crying and looked at him squarely in the eye. "I know what you're about to do. I'm begging you not do it. You don't need to kill my babies' mother just to get away. Killing me is an act of cruelty and completely unnecessary."

He nodded and continued to smile. "I know. Get out and walk away from the car. Hurry! Get into the trees as fast as you can. I won't kill you. I promise."

She stepped out and ran into the trees as fast as possible.

Bear lifted the automatic and fired straight into her back. He shot twice. She fell between the trees. He decided that she was out of sight of the highway enough for him to drive on. "Thanks for the car, sweetheart and thanks for the target practice!"

Satisfied with himself, he drove steadily to the next small town, and the next, which seemed larger. He found a motel and ditched the car three blocks further up the street by a drive-in that mostly advertised hamburgers.

Walking back to the motel he felt a slight chill in the afternoon breeze. The tops of pines wavering over the roofs of buildings acknowledged the wind from the mountains. The small city's planners built it on the side of a long slope. He liked what he saw. The city bordered a running river headed for a lower lake that hosted enough fish to last a lifetime for these people. He could go for a home like this.

He fumbled through cards in his wallet and found a real credit card in one of his many names, a good one not yet cancelled. He also found a driver's license that matched his name on the card. The mere thought of fitting into society provided a warm, comfortable feeling that soothed the aftermath of violence that occupied his other life. He needed to feel the security of everyday citizens that traveled about, all with sufficient funds in the bank. They could wander about a short while and then hurry home to get back to work the very next morning. He shuddered at the idea of thoughtless drudgery.

He spoke to the clerk at the motel desk. He knew that he would be asked what he was doing up in the mountains of West Virginia.

"I'm driving around enjoying what I see. My wife passed last year and I finally sold our house. I'd like to settle up here, you know, or something close to it."

The clerk nodded and smiled. "You and a lot of other people like these mountains. I'd ten times rather live here than anywhere out west. It feels like home here."

Bear liked the man. "Oh—we lived in Albuquerque a few years ago. That was a sweet city bordering a large mountain."

"What kind of work do you do?"

"I'm a radiologist. I work for a hospital in Richmond. It isn't difficult to get a job in my line of work, you know."

The clerk agreed. "I suppose not. It isn't everyone who has that kind of education. I can imagine that it's hard work with all that math and everything."

Bear nodded. "It's easy enough—hard enough!—too. I don't mind. It keeps the juices flowing in the old brain, you know."

The clerk lost interest in conversing once he knew the man behind the card seemed legitimate. He said, "Sign here, Dr. Tonklin."

In the clinic only four blocks away, Cody lay back on the cushioned bed while the local dentist examined his mouth. He washed it with foul smelling liquid and surveyed the equipment he had available. He looked up at the clinic's head nurse and said, "I'm going to transfer him to the hospital where I can work with better equipment. He's lost more blood than I like in order to do surgery. Move him by ambulance and order two pints of blood."

Cody looked up at his friends and shrugged. They both laughed at the large bandage covering his nose. Part of it also covered one eye. "I'm going to have to claim a few hours of sick leave, boss."

Leo glanced at Bob, who still couldn't help but grin. "Make him sign a release before he can come back for duty, boss."

Bob turned to Leo. "First, both you and Cody can stop calling me boss. I'm going to call Dan and bring him up to date. Cody will probably milk this for about six months or more just for light duty. The two of us probably can't handle what's coming. We are going to need dependable help."

Leo kept grinning and shook his head negatively. "I'm not worried about us not handling it, boss. Personally, I'm going on a couple of months' sick leave and see what it's like not being a prisoner to somebody. Cody's surgery is not as bad as the knot on the back of my head, by the way, and I'm not even milking it."

Two nurses loaded Cody in a chair and wheeled him outside where the ambulance waited.

Bob followed him, "Leo, you stay with Cody. I'll go find us a couple of rooms. He'll be in the hospital a day or two. I'll relieve you here after I check in and have a shower."

"Don't forget to call Dan after you find us a room. Cody and I are going to shop for some new duds. It's cold here without shirtsleeves."

Bob looked at him curiously. He failed to understand why Leo would cut the sleeves from a perfectly good shirt. Leo could be strange, sometimes. He drove a few blocks and found a motel on their road into town.

Once inside, the clerk looked at the plain, federal credit card. It seemed legitimate. "Two rooms, huh. Where's the other fella?

"Hospital. Bad accident."

The clerk nodded. "I appreciate the business. What's the federal government doing up here in our peaceful mountains?"

"We're of the Transportation Department, sir. The state wants money for some new roads. This is a routine trip."

"What do you guys do?"

Bob smiled at the man's curiosity. "Other than it being a boring story, I can tell you that we will travel every road in these parts and give your Congressman an unbiased report. That's about all we can discuss on the matter because there just ain't no more."

The clerk nodded and said with a great deal of skepticism. "Our tax dollars at work! I guess we can expect our state and federal taxes to go up."

"Not at all, sir. State and federal money are already appropriated. The area needing better roads will get the first attention."

The clerk said no more. Yet he couldn't shake the strange notion that the last man checking in fit somehow to this man, who appeared to be a curious type. Two men within the same hour raised his suspicions. Both of them had the same ready lies. Different lies, athletic types, same age group, single, and interested in anything but tourism or roads. They're connected! He thought.

After a shower and a clean change of clothes, Bob sat on the bed by the telephone and called the clerk. He told him that he wanted to call Bogota.

The clerk almost shouted. "I knew it! The other guy checking in just called Bogota! You guys are together! I can always tell!"

Bob jerked back as if suddenly snake bit. He thought of a hundred things at once and sat back. "Ohh—he's already called? Well, cancel mine. Thank you!"

Bob hurried downstairs. He found the idle clerk still smiling. He reached for his National Security badge and ID folder. "What room is my compatriot in?"

The clerk shook his head negatively. "That's not how it works, sir."

Bob shoved the phony credentials under the clerk's nose, who pulled back the same time Bob jerked them away and shoved them back into his hip pocket. "That's exactly how it works, sir! You give me the room number and I get to surprise your guest."

"Two—twelve, sir! I...er--I didn't get a good look at your badge."

"Yes, you did! Now—I'm going to cuff that guy and bring him down. If he runs before I get to his room, I'll know you called to warn him the police was on the way. You will simply go to jail. Clear?"

The unhappy clerk showed reluctance. "Clear."

Bob hurried upstairs and knocked on the door. A rough voice asked, "Who is it?"

"Room Service!" Bob answered pleasantly.

"This dump ain't got no room service! Go away or I'll kick you back down those stairs!"

Bob laughed loud enough to be heard. "It's usually flowers, grapes and apples! But you only get grapes and apples, sir!"

The voice uttered a couple of expletives and the door opened slightly.

Bob's fist shot straight for the man's face as soon as it appeared. He bumped the door that snapped the chain restraint the same time he followed through with a hard jab at the man's chest. The man's gun came up for protection. Bob kept low and kicked with his left leg in a flat arc. This caught the man's legs and put him on the floor belly up. Bob leapt forward in the air kicked directly into the man's face.

The fight had just begun for Bear. He acknowledged being suckered but he recovered quickly. The kick to his face hurt but he exchanged ends fast and kicked Bob in the middle, which slowed him. However, he needed his gun. It lay on the floor where he dropped it.

Bob spotted it first and kicked it under the bed and rushed Bear. That kept Bear on the floor, who blocked Bob's knee with his hands. Bob kicked the second time with more force while he held the back of Bear's head. The third time he kneed Bear in the face. The fight ceased. Bear dropped, completely unconscious.

Bob rolled him over and cuffed him. While Bear couldn't resist, Bob pulled on the handcuffs and placed a foot inside the chain. In the event Bear regained consciousness, this would give Bob a chance to meet him with an element of safety on his side. He used his thin tie to run under the handcuff's chain and around the ankle. After tying it to the handcuff chain and ankle securely, he relaxed and surveyed the room. If the man could escape this, he deserved his freedom. With that done, he picked Bear up and carried him to his own room. Without stopping, Bob opened the window with one hand and tossed Bear outside with the other. At two floors up, the fall could kill him, fine. If it merely crippled him, he wouldn't be leaving the premises as fast as he arrived.

He walked downstairs and moved his car as near as possible to his captive, who lay unconscious in the semi light covering the parking lot. Once the severely injured Bear lay crumpled inside Bob's trunk, he drove to the hospital--not to the emergency entrance.

CHAPTER 17

Leo used a flashlight to see Bear's face once they had safely arrived at an unpopulated area. He examined the mercenary long enough to find a bad gash on his forehead and a broken collar bone. He stopped and looked up to find Bob's face.

"I'm sorry, partner, but this man will live."

Bob's voice rasped as sad as Leo's. "I kind of doubt that."

Leo said with a certain amount of satisfaction. "You know, I had told Bear that if he ever found you that he wouldn't like it. Like other foolish people, he didn't believe me. Er...I don't like what we're going to have to do, Bob."

Bob nodded in the darkness. "It goes with the territory, Leo. We've been lucky on avoiding this sort of thing thus far."

"I don't like it but it is the only way," Leo stammered. "Bear was or is one hard core individual. That's all I care to say about him."

Bob asked with a brighter note, "How's Cody doing?"

"Cody is fast asleep while the dentist is using a hammer and chisel on the long root of an upper eye tooth. The doctor occasionally used a bad word. It doesn't look like Cody will be on his feet before tomorrow."

Bob no longer worried. "Let's finish this mess that you guys started."

Leo grimaced as Bear toppled a few feet down in the deep hole, his final resting place. He felt relief in knowing that Bear was no longer a threat to anyone else. He paused while leaning on his shovel's handle.

"You know, I don't mind giving this killer a burial instead of leaving him for the scavengers. He was going to bury us alive, while we were still breathing! Man—I hate to even think about that! He wouldn't have bothered to choke off our blood supply to our brains first. He was a psycho and that's his final, earthly epitaph."

They left the river's island where they buried Bear and found Bob's rental in the semi darkness. Bob carried the shovels and said, "I think that I'd like to sleep for a week."

"Go ahead. You need some rest before we arrive in Bogota."

"I hope that he was the last of the merks."

Leo assured him that Bear was the final one. He broke the shovel handles out of the metal necks and tossed all the remainder into the deeper part of the river.

On their way back to the hospital Leo looked at Bob. "This is it, Bob. Cody only came to find you at Dan's request. I only came because Cody threatened to toss me back into an Israeli jail if I didn't help find you. The mercenaries are dead and we have nowhere to go except Bogota."

"So what're you saying, Leo?"

"We're going to Bogota. That's what I'm saying! Bob, seriously, you're kind of dense."

The following morning in the motel, Cody awoke to pain in his mouth. He found the glass of water and pain medication the dentist set aside for Leo to give him. He swallowed two of them and read the label. He felt temporarily comforted in knowing that two tablets could be used in case of severe pain but only once each 12 hours. He looked at Leo. "I'm going home today."

Leo shook his head and talked toward the floor. "You know, Cody, you started that mess in Colombia and Bob and I bailed you out, well, mostly me. Bob usually stands by during these things. Now you want to turn it back to Bob and me to finish it by ourselves."

"I have a wife and kid, Leo. Ah--do you actually think that I wasn't joking?"

"I do with a great amount of understanding. It's just that the cartels will only hire more merks to come after us if we don't go down there and whip us up a peace treaty between them and us. You don't have to do anything, just keep Bob and mine's guns loaded."

Cody nodded and responded sadly. "You're right. I'm going home but I'll meet you guys in Dan's office Monday morning first thing."

Leo agreed. "You know that they may have a crew ready as we speak."

Cody brushed that aside. "They don't know that Bear and Horse are dead. That will give us some time."

Leo nodded negatively. "Bob said that Bear had already called Bogota. The only person they don't know is dead is Bear."

Cody thought a moment. "I think we will have plenty of time to meet in Bogota next Monday morning. We will be there before they can hire more people."

Bob walked back down to the motel clerk's office to give an explanation for Bear's disappearance. He said, "My quarry had split before I reached Room 212. Do you know anything about that?"

The clerk nodded uneasily. "I didn't call him, sir. You may think I did but I didn't. It ain't my fault that you missed 'im."

Bob held his hand up. "I believe you. Sometimes these guys have a sixth sense and know when we're close. I don't understand it."

The clerk said, "I run a clean place here. What did the guy do, anyhow?"

"He deserted while on leave from Vietnam a few years ago."

"Deserted? If I'd have known that I wouldn't have told you his room number. We never belonged over there, anyway, and we lost all those fighting men. It ain't right!"

"Yeah, I know," Bob said. "He deserted but not before he robbed a gas station and shot the attendant dead in his hometown in Alabama."

Oh—he planned to desert! Did he take off for the Alabama woods?"

"He did. We've chased him through the woods for almost a year. We got him this far before losing him again."

"Well, lots of luck on flushing him out of these woods. There are enough abandoned mines and caves around here to shelter him for a century."

Bob grinned. "We'll get 'im."

The clerk shrugged. "I hope you left my rooms in good shape and didn't steal my sheets and towels. Er...I'm joking trying to be friendly. I don't care about towels. Really!"

Bob climbed the stairs quickly and opened the door to Cody's room. All three men grinned at one another. Cody was grinning because he no longer suffered from a painful mouth. He even relished in talking through the hole the missing tooth made. He would have another built in Tucson.

"Hey, boss!" he said and pointed to Bob. "Thanks for giving Leo and me a hand in catching Bear! Good job! I'm proud of you!"

Bob glanced at Leo who was grinning and saying nothing. Bob knew that Cody was only having a backward attempt at humor. "So did Leo tell you that we closed his gate and locked it?"

"Yep! Leo said he was having a tough time getting the man under control until you came along and put the cuffs on him. Good enough. He got what was coming to him. So—if you kind gentlemen will excuse me, I'll be hopping a plane back to Tucson within this very hour."

"Don't leave until I talk with Dan and bring him up to date." Bob sat back down and began the procedures in calling Bogota.

Cody lay back down and held a cold rag to his mouth. "Those pain killers haven't been swallowed an hour and they have just about lost their potency."

Leo sat up straight and began in his favorite type of dry humor for the day. "You can't have my aspirin. It'll thin your blood and make you bleed."

Cody groaned but delighted in some of Leo's good spirits.

Dan said, "All three of you get over here now and clean that nest of vipers out. I already have the president's permission but that, gentlemen, is to remain a secret. If his army catches you, me or the president has never heard of you. You might want to remember that."

Bob hesitated, "Yeah, we remember, but it'll make a good book in a few years. By the way, Cody needs to get back home. Let's cut him some slack. Leo and I will handle it."

Dan almost yelled. "He gave you guys the same sob story? Look, I doubt if he even has a girlfriend, far less of being married with a toddler. Let me talk to him."

Dan greeted Cody politely then said, "You want to go home? Are you quitting before you have one more round with the well-armed cartels outside of town?"

Cody replied, "Why no! Are you believing everything these guys tell you? But...you don't remember that I'm not even getting paid for helping find Bob? Leo told me that you had put him in charge. I worked my socks off keeping Leo out of trouble and alive! Now you're telling me that I can't go home or be the boss one time in my short career?"

Dan responded with a word of caution, "Cody, retroactively, you're fully reinstated."

"Okay, boss, but I'm still going home today and will be in your office Monday morning and do not put Leo in charge of me ever again!"

Dan said, "I would never do that! Don't you believe him if he tells you differently. You know what? You guys give me a headache!"

Cody said, "Well, anyway, after this caper, I've had it with this lousy detail!"

"Dan said, "Stop hanging out with Leo so much before I put you both back on probation! Put Bob on the telephone!"

Cody stopped grinning. "Here's Bob. He eats this management and supervisory stuff up if you don't know that, already."

Bob picked up the receiver and said, "We'll catch a bus to Richmond and fly out of there today, hopefully." He slammed the telephone against its cradle in hopes of beating Dan to it.

Bob looked at Leo. "Okay, Homie, you're in charge of this mission."

Leo jumped. "Me? How about Cody? Didn't he say that Cody could be in charge for even a little while?"

Bob and Cody both nodded negatively.

"Okay! Um," Leo stammered. "We'll ride the bus to Richmond and fly out of there today. Ah...Why can't we put Cody in charge?"

Bob whisked the idea away with his right hand. "Cody is still on probation."

Leo's eyes still showed shock and surprise. "Oh—yeah! With me in charge, I doubt if he ever gets off it."

CHAPTER 18

The full time lawyer hired by the Rubio Organization hung up the telephone. He paused a second and turned back to the owners, an elderly man, overweight with a heavy, white mustache to match his head of white hair. His two sons appeared bored, both fortyish and well dressed. All three listened as their lawyer spoke in a rich, Castilian tongue, proud of his Spanish heritage, educated in Barcelona and the University of Bogota.

"Gentlemen," he said, "I have lost my faith in the two Americans we hired to rid ourselves of the three private detectives. The newspaper in the West Virginia town of Cagney tells of a stranger only known as Horse died in a vehicle and tree accident yesterday. I haven't heard anything more from the one called Bear since yesterday. I fear that he has taken our money and disappeared in the face of adversity."

The elder Rubio lifted a hand and said, "We should never have hired them. We should leave the United States alone. We don't need to add to their hatred of us. I say let matters alone. We will suffer our loss with a lesson well learned."

One son disagreed, the one with the deepest frown lines between his eyebrows. "Popa, with just a little more force in the right places, we could own that country like we own Colombia. Think of the money we would earn! We would have our own president to rule that country after I stripped President Reagan naked and forced him to walk a bed of blazing coals until he dropped. Then I would have a handful of women to hack him to tiny pieces with machetes and let the tiny pieces roast over the coals."

The elder Rubio dreaded to hear such words. He closed both eyes into a tight squint while nodding negatively and waving both aged hands over his broad chest and stomach. "No-no-no, Rafael! Too violent! We must leave that country in peace! Tell him, Antonio, tell your brother that he is wrong, that we must never attempt to be larger than what we are!"

Antonio relished in his time to speak. "My father, Rafael is correct. Why rob ourselves of riches and power? We could be kings of the world once we rule that great country! No country in the world would dare attack us with that large military and with the finest weapons in the world! That could all be ours."

The lawyer stood up and held both hands out for silence. "Gentlemen, please! You brothers are young and full of ambition. Your father and uncle are pleased with the both of you. Let us not forget that your father is the great and mighty Patriarch of the large Rubio Clan. Brothers, he has willed everything to you! Let him have his wishes while he lives!"

"Yes—yes! My beloved attorney! Tell them of my desire to love and care for my great family! We educate the young and support them in their causes. They will be pleased to know they can take this great business to new heights! There are no limits for the Rubio family!"

The lawyer stood and voiced his opinion with respect and clarity. "Gentlemen, Moscow was receptive and welcomes me there as soon as I can arrive. We no longer need the common mercenaries to rid ourselves of the three thorns in our sides. We will fight fire with fire. I will hire the best that Russia has to offer. While America has these three men that amount to super heroes, I will hire one man who is a far greater super hero!"

"And who is this great Russian that can accomplish what four fighting men could not?" one of the brothers asked.

"Alexander Kroschov, this Olympian gymnast has mastered three marital arts. Gentlemen, he is probably the most unfeeling, arrogant and dangerous man in the world. He maims men in the ring and laughs!"

Rafael's eyes brightened. "Is this the fighter who brags that he wants to kill men in the kick boxing events? You know, the one called Sasha Kroschov?"

The lawyer smiled. "He is and he's happy to know that he's free to kill all three of these men who has come to our country to harass us. He wants them chained or in a cage where they cannot escape. No professional fighter or wrestler in Russia or Japan will fight him. They claim he is a maniac that needs to be imprisoned."

The elder Rubio held up his hand. "How much are we paying this Russian fighter?"

The lawyer smiled. "I have offered a flat payment of three million dollars equivalence in Russia for the death of these three men. I will fly to Moscow and put him under contract with important men witnessing the verbal deal."

Senor Rubio nodded negatively. "That is a lot of money for one man."

The lawyer laughed. "By the time he leaves the Kremlin within an hour of his payment, he will probably have earned one tenth of that payment just by instilling fear into people, sir."

All of the Rubios smiled and nodded. The elder said, "The east is learning fast."

"Okay, boss," Bob said as they flew out of Richmond to New York. "Have you worked out a strategy to accomplish our mission outside Bogota?"

"First of all, Bob," Leo began, "we have never have had a plan yet. So back off! Me leader. You pest. I lead by action, so remember that while you're trying to keep up with me. That's my plan!"

Bob threw both hands into the air. "Oh—Man!—we're in trouble."

Leo's humor broadened at Bob's assertion of his leadership. He said, "Hey, partner, don't set your pants on fire! You want details, don't you? Okay, listen up, I've listened to all this time with a new record of boredom."

They stretched and yawned, then settled back in their chairs while Leo sat anxiously. He said, "I'll send in Cody first to scout. On his way in he can take o ut the guards. Are you with me thus far, Bob? I don't like having to repeat myself. As I was saying, Cody can take out the guards and the heavyweights inside. I'd rather he didn't use firepower but we cannot determine that until the time comes. I had rather use diplomacy instead of his guns. I'm sure these folks are reasonable people."

Bob looked in the other direction. "I'm sure Cody will eat this plan up."

"Okay," Leo said impatiently. "Enough chatter from the monkey section. We already know the lay of the land. Cody needs to take a little extra ammo inside with him in case he needs it. He'll take care of everyone on the inside and start working his way back out again. After he eliminates the main threat, he can run all the workers off and burn the place down. We can back him from our position in the trees. Cody will then steal us an airplane and we'll fly to the next cartel. Any questions?"

Bob said, "There are two cartels that have sworn vengeance against us. The Rubios and the Montiago Cartel. Which one do we do first?"

Leo shrugged, "I'll get to that! I deem the same plan for both of them. Do you have any more dumb questions?"

Bob shook his head negatively. "Cody might not like it but it sounds okay to me."

Leo brushed it aside. "Cody uses far too much sick leave. I'll deny all his requests for that nonsense."

Bob said, "I think that I want about two weeks of leave right now!"

"Denied!" Leo said firmly. "No one in this club can claim sick or annual leave."

Bob responded more seriously. "I'm checking in with our union leader tomorrow to see about having you removed from office."

Monday. They arrived by taxi by the time Dan arrived to open the office. One of Dan's D.E.A. agents, however, happened to beat Dan to the office. At first he watched at a distance before recognizing the Leo and Bob. Cody arrived by another taxi in time for the three to enter Dan's office together.

After many greetings to everyone, Dan called all the agents in whether they worked another shift or had days off. He wanted to celebrate a reunion that he never expected to happen in his lifetime. The three had done more than any officers working before them and had lasted longer, and they still had a mission remaining. Dan retired before he had spent this much time in the field and considered himself fortunate to be alive. A celebration filled the air and festivity leapt from person to person.

Dan sent the women in a seized car for all the sweet bread they could find. They returned with a large box of sweet bread, a large sack of fruit and an extra pound of coffee. He felt genuine fear for his three remaining agents on this mission and he prayed it wouldn't be their last.

Before they could get a word in, Dan talked above everyone. "I never thought to see all three of you together again. I am free to tell you that you have the president's blessing to wipe out any and all ranches at your discretion, but he understands the Rubio and Montiago Cartels have to go first. He doesn't care if you bomb them or burn them. But if you get caught by anybody, by law enforcement or the cartels, you are on your own. All of your past deeds of harassing his army have been forgiven. You guys really needed to come here in a U. S. Customs jet in order to avoid the airport. Did the port authorities suspect you any at all?"

"Dan, we don't fly in Customs jets if Cody is at the controls!" Leo said. Bob dittoed the remark.

Dan appeared puzzled, along with Cody and the remainder of the Bogota crew. He wore a genuine worried expression. "I thought he had gone to school and learned how to fly. You guys are always joking."

Cody felt the urge to raise his hand to remind everyone of his presence.

Leo shook his head negatively and threw up his hands. "Flight school? Oh it helped. Cody can crash much more safely now than he used to without any training. He's about as safe at the controls of an airplane as a hundred year-old stick of sweating TNT."

Cody grinned and said, "If you're through making me feel bad for keeping you guys safe in Iraq, I'm having one more doughnut and flying myself home without you. That is, if Dan will loan me another one of his seized aircraft."

Everyone laughed at that remote possibility. Bob spoke up. "Dan, could you please arm us? I'm feeling naked in Colombia without at least two side arms and an assault rifle. Give Cody and Leo a couple of slingshots and a few boxes of ammo to carry for me. They never use their firepower, anyway."

Dan, who could never get used to their strange humor, turned away and led them to a portable vault. Cody found two .357 revolvers and searched for a third. Leo and Bob found two 10 millimeters with large grips.

"Are they all sighted in?" Cody asked.

Dan nodded affirmatively. "They do that at the factory with computer science during these times. They're precise."

Bob grinned. Leo liked the feel of his automatic. Cody placed one revolver under his belt and the other inside his belt at the back. Dan turned to them and said, "All three of you can have holsters for goodness sakes! This isn't U.S. Customs, you know."

Downstairs they found a short, one-man firing range with small paper targets. "Forget this," Bob said. "We'll fine tune them out of town somewhere."

Cody grinned. "Just point, Bob, because we won't have the time to aim."

Bob frowned. "If I didn't aim, Cody, you wouldn't be here."

"You're right!" Leo said. "Let's find somewhere outside of town to sight these suckers in the way they're supposed to be. Dan, lend us some practice ammo. We'll need four rounds each, except for Cody. He don't need any practice because he's too scared, political-wise, to ever use his sidearm."

Dan replied, "You guys will have an old car and all the ammo I can spare. There's no paperwork on the car so don't get caught by the police or army. Each of you will have one box of practice ammo. Use it. You came back for more after the company sends me a fresh supply. In other words, make your shots count."

Leo shook his head. "Well, I guess we can forget cover fire. The Department of Justice must be paying for the ammo. Cheapskates!"

"Whatever," Bob said. "There will be no cover fire. If we make each shot count, we'll only come out with about 1,000 rounds short. We'll be hand to hand in no time and outnumbered and, thanks to Leo's lousy humor, outwitted."

Dan said, "Okay, guys! That's enough of your grumpy old women's small talk. The President of Colombia wants to meet you. We will have dinner with him at seven this very evening. Be ready to leave from here at six-thirty."

Count me out!" Leo said. "I don't want to be known by your friends in high places."

Cody said, "I'll be in Tucson by six-thirty this evening."

Bob shook his head sadly. "I'll be out in the field ambushing cartel members, so I can't make it."

"Okay, ladies. I'm warning you that it ain't smart to disappoint the President of Colombia. I'll have to lie for you. It won't be as easy for you this time. You may need a few friends in high places before this is over."

CHAPTER 19

Sasha Kroschov arrived in Richmond's International Airport and passed through Customs and Immigration with hardly slowing. He noticed two men walking to the tunnel in order to embark. They appeared familiar from old snap shots. Their names, of course, could be learned later. He couldn't believe his luck! He checked the schedules and found the two flying for Bogota. He wondered at their decision to die so quickly. He attempted to board the same plane and found it impossible. He had to wait another twenty-four hours before the next flight. He dreaded the delay but remained thankful that he had found two targets so fast. The third couldn't be far away.

At his hotel room, he skipped dinner and went straight into his exercise routine without weights or machines for one hour. He rested with more push-ups. Again, he congratulated himself on being so fortunate. He read names aloud from the telephone directory to practice his English. The Spanish names came easy. He also congratulated himself on his superior intellect and advanced education classes. Perhaps his major study should have been foreign languages instead of martial arts but not half the fun.

He considered the idea of remaining in the United States in order to become rich and famous like others with superior physiques. He could beat any of them and become a champion in their puny fighting games. He felt the steel muscles in his arms and legs, gently caressing them as he smiled in the mirror. Huge amounts of money could be made in the United States and China with muscles such as his. He would fly to Bogota, and call one of the cartels. He didn't remember which but it didn't matter to him. He would finish this easy assignment, and then fly back to Atlanta where he would begin his new career in fighting professionally. The United States of America loved athletes such as himself.

Leo sat in their car parked in front of the office. Inside an hour the three of them would be walking through the trees and thick brush to the old headquarters of what used to be known as The Growling Cat Ranch. The present Rubio owners had rebuilt it and turned it into a profitable cocaine business without the animal cages.

Rosa, he knew, had made it profitable for the General of the Colombian Army who would and did become the President of Colombia. He seized it upon Rosa's death in order to sell it to other enterprising individuals whose son had married the President's sister.

The president didn't care for the man who married his sister, whom he loved as he did his mother. She and the eldest Rubio son grew rich fast and this seemed to be the way of cartels. The president personally wanted to kill the cartels, which would make him one of the most popular Colombian Presidents, a national hero in several countries. Of course, he planned to sacrifice his sister's ranch along with many more. She wouldn't approve, but she must appreciate the good of her country. However, she would soon be listed as one of the Colombia's richest widows with her picture seen often in the periodicals. That would be a good thing for her since she has always been beautiful.

During this time the United States swingers among the norm would be starving for cocaine. Mexico and the shallow-led countries south of it would be eager to do business with him. Once the cocaine producers were officially nationalized, he would rapidly become the richest and most powerful man in the western hemisphere, perhaps, the world!

To Leo's prediction, the three men walked through the heat and continually sprayed themselves with flying insect repellant. It came off with the sweat in the humid atmosphere. Bob stopped at the first clearing and sat at the base of a large tree. Thousands of gnats circled his head but refused to land due to the repellent. Ants from the tree made a new trail around him.

Without talking, Cody and Leo found their own trees for a backrest. Cody had taught them to keep their voices to a whisper and listen to all sounds. In no time they will have learned the natural sounds of the forest. All the unnatural sounds would reach the wildlife and could possibly result in much noise, putting the entire forest on alert. Such noise would also alert the guards surrounding cocaine plantations. They, too, would respond in their own manner.

The trio walked slowly and lightly, careful not to allow limbs to scrape across their thick denim pants. No slaps to the face and no coughing or sneezing allowed, according to Cody. They welcomed their first break in the high humidity. Both Bob and Leo frowned in Cody's direction each time he uttered an outdoor rhetoric.

Leo even rolled his eyes upward when Cody whispered loudly to them to keep their chit chat down. Cody crawled to Leo and told him of an approaching rain storm. Leo turned away and sighed loudly as if Cody didn't exist.

Cody them crawled to Bob, who quickly waved him away. Cody Loved it.

They waited another ten minutes before hearing thunder. Once the rain arrived, Cody made a large leaf into a funnel and passed it to his friends. Nothing quenched thirst like cool rain falling from high clouds. Cody emptied his canteen and used the funnel to refill it. The two others followed suit but the rain stopped abruptly the moment they drained their canteens. They both glared at him with contempt. He smiled and patted his canteen. Their rain-drenched clothes also proved discomforting. Cody had no ideal in how to get their minds off their present state of affairs.

They walked another six miles before Cody lifted his fist to stop. He pointed to two large trees and began climbing one of them. Leo and Bob watched from below, their skeptic volumes turned up to max. He motioned for them to follow. Cody could see the red tops of buildings less than a half-mile away. He pointed to them and found a huge fork in the limbs where he sprawled inside. It would be his bed for the night. Leo climbed downward in order to find his bed. Bob found a nice fork in the limbs. They rested without complaint, which Cody interpreted as peace with his two comrades. It rained again in the middle of the night.

The following morning Cody climbed down and found both Bob and Leo waiting silently at the base of their tall tree, both stiff. Tension filled the air. He drew close to them and whispered, "Good Morning!"

Leo scowled at him. Bob said nothing. "Did you sleep well?" he asked in a low whisper.

He received two harsh negatives. Cody nodded. "It's okay. It usually takes one or two nights before you can really sleep."

He received more harsh frowns. Cody felt good about it, *another good assignment starting out well.*

Sasha arrived in Bogota that morning instead of having to wait another twelve hours as expected. He called the Montiago lawyer for his first item of business. Once he made the call he sat in the hotel lobby and waited for the car that would carry him to the fabulous residence. The Montiago lawyer alerted all the cocaine cartels and those growing marijuana that the foreign guerrillas had returned to Bogota. All responded positively and on full alert.

Sasha arrived in time for lunch at the Montiago mansion. They provided him a warm welcome. He responded with an array of shabby Spanish amid his arrogant attitude. The man claimed to be a linguist as well as a martial arts expert. He seemed intent on murdering his hosts' language. He not only proved to be a braggart to the Montiagos, not to mention the arrogance. He interrupted others who talked, an ill gesture never practiced in traditional Spanish households. The elder Montiago excused himself into the kitchen and instructed the chef to double the hot but delicious *jalapeños*.

In mid-meal, Sasha turned silent and motioned for more water.

The brothers showed Sasha his room and invited him to the pool. They presented him several choices of swim wear. Sasha chose the smallest piece in order for the females to admire more of his muscular body. The brothers excused themselves and retired to the many shades surrounding the large pool.

Sasha strangely found that no woman offered to keep him company. He used the diving board several times but still no female attempted to catch his attention. Deeply offended, he resigned himself to his room early that afternoon. He also skipped dinner. He found relief in exercising and kept it up until bedtime.

Cody led his troops halfway to the Rubio headquarters but a machine gun suddenly stopped them. He felt confident they didn't see him but suspected their arrival somehow. Gunfire erupted from both to their left and right. Bullets soon hit the underbrush surrounding them and imbedded into the trees they each huddled against. They finally realized that the shooter fired blindly to discourage anyone if they arrived from the forest. They wasted a lot of bullets for a show of strength. One automatic weapon opened up directly south of them not more than fifty yards distant! Each of the three remained unmoved. Bullets continued to pop through the leaves. The shooter called out for the three terrorists to show themselves and surrender.

Leo stared at Cody and questioned him by opening his hands as if what to do. Cody grinned and motioned for Leo to hold his hands in the air. All three had to chuckle at the suggestion.

He put a finger to his lips. They had their weapons ready. Then another burst of machine gun fire reached them from their left. New sentries followed suit further away. They all shot blind, attempting to scare off any intruders by yelling insults and firing into the brush. *A bluff, worse, an unproven bluff!* They had received word that the enemy had arrived. How?

Cody wondered while his partners scowled at him, knowing no one to blame but Cody. Cody never got mad, a good man! Cody kept his focus on matters at hand. They knew of no one being in the area. He suspected they would keep this up for most of an hour, shooting into the brush, running their bluffs to the fullest. They heard more shooting further to their left. No doubt, heavily armed sentries surrounded the entire plantation.

Both men frowned at Cody when the shooting stopped. One of the sentries could not be far out of earshot. Cody signed for them to wait. They both looked at each other nodded their heads sadly. *This mission had suddenly turned into a hummer.*

An hour after the blind and wasteful shooting, the sentries of the former Growling Cat Ranch had satisfied themselves that they had thoroughly discouraged an attack by foreign terrorists if they were there. This was only their first day under the threat of an attack.

Then the rain came. Cody bounded over to the next tree where Bob stood. Leo jumped the entire distance between him and Bob just to see if he could.

They communicated in whispers. Both Cody and Leo watched behind the tree. Bob watched behind them. "I think that they really believed we are here." Leo whispered.

Bob said, "Someone gave us away. Was it the president, perhaps?"

Cody nodded, "Someone did for sure. Maybe we should have accepted his invitation to dinner."

"Ladies, what *shall* we do?" Bob asked as sarcastic as possible. "The options are to continue with the attack on the facility or else walk back to town. We are presently unable to attack these machine guns. This is the first sign of our intellect. We still have the sensible solution to hoof it back to the car with our tails between our legs."

Cody spoke up more firmly than ever. "I'm doing no more walking! Period! In fact, I'm going to rest for at least a couple days. This way, the cartels will believe their information was false."

Leo favored that option. "Rest is healthy for the body."

Bob whispered, "Then let's find our trees, boys. They won't hear us with this rain."

Dan sat idly in his office waiting for anything to happen. The president broke the silence by calling to ask if he had heard anything from his new troops. Dan wondered at the man's sudden enthusiasm. *"This is not the president I know!"*

Dan figured that his official friend wanted most of the cartels broken up in order to prove to the United States that he was using their donated money wisely. The *mordida* (bite) from the cartels willing to share their profits with the president did nothing but fatten his wallet. He didn't care about any of them. Once the president eventually established a tax system, he promised to rid the entire country of illegal activities. He loved a capitalist system but he planned to remain in power forever.

"In the meantime," Dan mused, "Cody could go home and Leo would soon be bound for the Bahamas."

Bob, he knew, if he survived this mission, would either return to Memphis for good or spend his few remaining years working in Bogota. He sighed. Without Lucy, nothing mattered. Whatever they decided would work for him.

Cody knew that he would have his hands full keeping Leo occupied for the next two days, so he decided to forget rest and attack immediately. He should have insisted earlier to attack the large, automatic weapons, each with hundreds of rounds of ammo. He inhaled a large lungful of air and released it slowly. Bob would, no doubt, remain in his state of depression indefinitely if he didn't do something soon. He glanced briefly at Bob who seemed to simmer in sadness as if it could be his private place of security. Perhaps he would help keep Leo's mind occupied if they began their work.

Time passed slowly while Cody pondered his issue. They grew sleepy and Cody saw Bob eventually drop his chin.

Suddenly, both Cody and Leo jumped when Bob burst out of silence in a loud voice. "I will never settle down with that woman!"

Cody grabbed his chest to save his heart from jumping from it. Leo's mouth had fallen open and he finally whispered, "I'm glad we got that cleared up!"

Cody asked, "Are you guys ready?"

Leo asked, "Do you mean if I'm ready to commit suicide?"

Cody grinned and whispered, "That depends upon whether or not you return their fire."

"That would be my line for you, partner."

CHAPTER 20

The surprise of the day for the station chief for the DEA in Bogota came in the form of a telephone call from a stranger. Dan listened closely, not really believing what he heard. A man who called himself Sasha had dialed him.

"Tell your three cowardly American friends that I have come to kill them with my bare hands, one at a time or all three. I do not care!"

Dan said, "Listen, friend, you are either out of your mind or drunk. I know nothing of men who are cowards. I have my own team working here. Now who are you and where are you?"

Sasha laughed heartily. "I am never drunk! I have perfectly sound faculties and your three men are, indeed, cowards. I reside at Senor Montiago's head household near Medellin. Where else would I get your number, since your place of business is the most popular in Bogota? Tell your men to come. Tell them they have no fear of being shot by guards. I—alone— will meet them without arms. They will have their freedom if they can defeat me! I am Sasha Kroschov!"

"I'm sorry, Mr. kashmahoof, you have the wrong number."

"Kroschov, you dumb American! You tell them the message I have given you or I will kill you for free!"

"Go find your mother's lap in Russia, punk. Stay off my telephone before I look you up, myself!" Dan slammed the receiver down.

"The nerve of some people!" he exclaimed and dialed his friend, the president.

"Hello, Dan! Good morning to you, my friend! How..."

"Stuff it, Mr. President!" Either you or someone alerted the cartels that my men are here. In fact..."

"Hold on, Dan!"

"No—you hold on, Mr. President. Some Russian scumbag just called me on my telephone and threatened my three men!"

The president came across genuinely astounded. "Dan, believe me. I would never double cross you! It behooves me to have you as a friend. Could it be possible that the leak came from your office?"

"No. The timing is way off. Someone in your office knows my number and what we have planned. Do you have a bug in your telephone?"

"Why—Dan! Do not think I would betray our friendship. I will call you back after we sweep my office."

Dan hung up and checked his temper. He sat down and began to worry. NOT GOOD! Without the president's friendship, the cartels would kill his entire office and their families.

Three minutes later, the president dialed him directly. "Yes, you are right, my friend. I found the device in my telephone. I cannot believe it! I always do the sweeps regularly!"

Dan reassured him. "I trust you. It was such a shock to have that stupid Russian calling me like that. I have no way of reaching my men."

"Dan," the president said, "Let's talk again when I have all the bugs swept from my office. Someone is going to prison over this!"

Dan fretted over having no way of warning Bob and his crew about some ego-filled Russian that's works for the cartels. But the flip side of it was that the Russian will have his own surprise when he started something with Leo or the other two. He needed to warn his men but had no choice but to let nature take its course. He needed to tell his men to not accept any type of challenge from that lunatic. He wanted to personally snatch all three by the collar and tell them to bomb all the ranches processing cocaine.

He approached one of the secretaries. "Leo will make short work of that Russian!"

The lady looked up in surprise. "What Russian, Dan? You still have those guys on your mind, don't you?"

Dan nodded and eased away. "I'm sorry. Sometimes my thoughts come out in words. I'll work on that."

She understood. "This has to do with that telephone call that made you angry, isn't it? Have no worries, Dan. Your men are the best you can find."

He stopped and agreed. "I know but they are not indestructible! Something else is riding on this operation. If my men go down, we will follow, all of us. In fact, the entire nation is already in big trouble. I need to be with them."

She almost rose to her feet with her voice more firm than anytime she used it at work. "No—you should not be with them! The reason that you didn't send the entire team with them is because they work better alone. If they wanted you they would have asked. Now please go somewhere else to do your worrying. I have my work!"

Another agent stepped within hearing distance and fired a serious warning at Dan with his eyes. Dan attempted to ignore him but failed. He attempted to stifle a chuckle. The agent noted this and chuckled.

Dan stepped into another room and sat down.

They decided to launch their attack after a good meal. They ate from their packs and drank rain water.

Cody spoke first. "I started this mess a long time ago because these radical drug smugglers abducted my wife. You guys really aren't obligated to do anything but get yourselves back to town and find yourselves a decent life. Live it. I'm saying this for the first time. I detect faint, volcanic-type explosions within my shaky and extremely questionable nervous system. I'll make it simple. I sense danger."

Leo spoke up. "So what are you saying, Cody?"

Bob spoke up, "He's just being fearful, Leo. Cut 'im some slack."

Leo almost chuckled. "Oh? Scared? Is that it? Facing a battle for the first time, are you? Not to worry, my nervous little probationer, it will pass."

Bob enjoyed Leo's teasing for the first time in weeks. "I agree, Cody. It will pass after a bullet shatters your kneecap or passes through your heart. You'll be fine."

Leo said, "Bob, have a little empathy."

Cody felt exasperated. "I'm sorry, guys, but the fear wasn't for me, it was for you."

"Oh—that!" Leo blurted out. "Well, that's different! Let's take this thing a little slower and do a little more planning. What say you, Bob?"

"I say if I hear another word out of either one of you, I'm hoofing it back to town and let you two go in alone."

"I'm quiet." Cody said.

"Me, too." Leo added.

Cody paused only a moment, then said, "This is not the right thing to do, guys. For the three of us to go in there is nothing but suicide. We've beaten the odds before, sure, but suicide is not the Christian way. I'm not a good one, but I'm a believer. Suicide is for the heathen. Besides, if that great Colombian president wants these people out of business, he's got the army to put them out. Our job obligations are nothing but a deadly game played by monsters and politicians. I'm all for packing it all in if you guys are with me."

Bob said, "It's twelve miles back to town, Cody!"

Cody said, "We have walked that far before, I think. Haven't we?"

"No." Bob said. "Besides, I don't see how you can walk with your sore mouth. We have hiking boots. You wear cowboy boots! Your feet and mouth must be killing you as we speak."

"Bob, for your information, good cowboy boots fit like a pair of socks. I can stand on a half-inch iron bar all day in these boots. All I have to do is stand with the bar next to the heel. The weight is distributed to the front and back evenly. The arch support is built around a large nail that's bent toward the angle of your foot while standing. You won't feel the bar for it will be no different from standing on a flat surface, unless, of course, you get unbalanced. They're expensive but I never have to worry about blisters or tired feet. In fact, I really can't tell I even have them on except when I take them off."

Leo stood up and walked passed Cody, dropping a hand on his shoulder. "Terrific. Let's do our job before we have to listen to another lecture about your stinking feet?"

Cody sighed, "We're going to be short on ammo."

Bob asked, "How much did you pay for those kickers, anyway?"

"About three--hundred bucks more than you paid for those enclosed sandals that you call hiking boots."

Bob grinned and stood up. "Okay, ladies, let's try and do the mission before Christmas."

They stopped one hundred yards passed where they witnessed hundreds of wasted rounds from their enemies earlier. Upon hearing nothing but regular sounds, they pushed on toward the huge cartel residence and manufacturing sheds. Sporadic gunfire could be heard as each sentry took his turn at shooting into the brush from different positions. Cody looked up at the sun and squinted. He wished for ammo to waste like their opponents.

He whispered, "Okay, guys, we'll hit them from the east end of this oblong circle with the sun at our backs. Let's split into three attack positions. Waste no rounds and shoot anyone within firing distance."

Leo asked him, "Are you or are you not putting in for sick leave before we go in?"

Cody said, "If we have a choice and not over-run, the man on the left shoots first. When he slacks off, the middle man fires, and then it's the third man's turn. We should last longer that way."

"Good thinking, Cody." Leo said. "Please do not run over a mile to the right while waiting your turn."

"I'm in the middle." Cody said firmly. "Leo, you're our left man. Just try and point the barrel of your gun toward the bad guys and not at your feet."

Bob said, "I have something to say, gents. We have to find cover fast. The big house is at the west end. We go in on each side of the house. Two go on the heaviest side. It doesn't matter to me. We really need to take that house and rid ourselves of the bodyguards! They will also be shooting at us from all around it."

"Is that all?" Leo asked.

"Yes. Leo, you may have the floor."

"Okay, as I see it, I don't think the three of us can enter that place without catching a bullet or two. If only one of us catches a bullet, then it will be a miracle. In other words, Bob, if I don't make it and you two do, do *not* allow Cody to make probation. He's no good if he's not oppressed with hoof and mouth disease. Hear me out, now. I have been to a few places, ladies. Sadly, I have never seen the Bahamas. Well, what I want to tell you two is that it has been my pleasure to work with both of you. No joke. I'm serious for the first time in my life."

Cody and Bob said, "Ditto!" at the same time. They bumped one another's fists.

Before they split, Cody asked Leo, "Not to get all blubbery again but I have to know one thing. Seriously, will you guys ever fly with me again? Really, that means a lot to me."

Leo almost shouted, "That's a major negative!"

Bob added, "You just soured the good feelings I had for you, Cody. I cannot believe that you would ask that of us."

"Thanks, guys." Cody said sadly. "I feel much better now."

Leo took the far right. Bob chose the middle and Cody, feeling hurt, accepted the left side. He guessed that he was near the left edge of the oval. In no time the sentry in Leo's position fired into the brush toward him and yelled for help. Leo silenced the man with one round. Several shooters answering the call rushed at Leo's position. They came *en mass*. Cody heard shots from Bob before he joined in, one shot at a time. Men had already begun to fall as fast as the three men could shoot.

The firing stopped momentarily while the attackers regrouped. Another group of men rushed Bob's position in the brush. Cody moved closer to Bob. A sentry suddenly appeared in front of Cody, who dived for a tree and pressed against it, feeling it vibrate from the heavy balls of lead striking it. A lead pellet traveling at a thousand feet per second bears a heavy impact. The brush around him shattered as if an invisible buzz saw cut through it. Cody silently reaffirmed his opponents had superior weapons.

Bob fired from the brush and Cody's attacker quickly attempted to disappear around a building. Cody aimed for the man's back and fired straight for the center of it. The shooter dropped. Another man showed with an automatic weapon. Cody shot him the moment he appeared and dove to recover the man's rifle with a large clip. They definitely needed more guns.

He looked about for others and continued toward Bob's position. He watched the building from the corner of his eye, hoping to find a door. Bob received heavy fire from inside the terrace of the huge building. Cody used the automatic weapon until the slide stopped suddenly. He turned back with his big revolver from the back of his belt. He saw lots of men but chose those that posed the most dangerous position. They stormed the area where he had shot the others. He continued to fire from his flank position, counting his shots and dreading the outcome.

With the last few rounds in both revolvers almost gone, he spent them on the two men running toward him. Time to reload!

Three of them went down from Bob, who really didn't need to aim. He dropped the last man while the others retreated. Angry and scared, Bob pointed his sidearm carefully and dropped one more man. His slide stopped open. He dropped the empty clip and slid another in its place. He could not reload again. He came into this firefight with only forty-eight rounds. His next two targets ran toward him. He dropped on his belly and had grass cover until the men drew closer and dropped. Two more precious rounds spent.

Cody stared at his own sidearm, a six-shooter, way out of date! He wished for another automatic rifle.

No other men showed. Leo ran to Bob in the brush. Much of it had been cut away next to the perimeter. He heard Bob make an occasional shot. He called Bob's name before dropping to his stomach behind him. The firing ceased.

Cody asked both of them, "Do you have any of their assault rifles and any ammo for them?"

Both answered negatively. Cody raised and spotted no one. "Okay, we move with our personal weapons. Be accurate! I don't want to be shot in the back by a wounded sentry."

Leo sighed. "Sooner or later, Cody, you're going to have to shoot someone, yourself. I'm all out!"

Bob spoke up. "Knock it off, Leo! The west gate is to our right in that fence. Run low and use the fence. If we don't move now, we're dead. I'm sure they'll be coming next to the fence from our left and right. Let's find cover inside the gate and wait for them."

They filed through the gate one at a time and found cover in the grass on both sides of it. Bob dove into it. He would be firing to his left and right.

Cody couched down within a few feet of the gate. He hesitated and realized the ringing in his ears grew steadily louder. *Actually,* he thought, *how could they still be fighting without catching a bullet?* Their attackers thinned out and many ran back to the buildings. These people didn't act like professional guards. They acted like workers. He gritted his teeth against this new fact. *This explained why not one of them caught a bullet!*

The owners used the workers as a force as if there was such a thing as safety in numbers. "Not good!" he said aloud and ran toward the downed sentries. Upon seizing three rifles, he ran back to his friends. Bullets ricocheted off the hard surface on each side of him.

CHAPTER 21

Cody could hear men shouting and running on his left side but far inside the compound.

Leo could hear men approaching fast from his left. They hugged the inside of the fence. All three rose and fired several times with the new weapons before dropping down again. While on his stomach, Cody reloaded his revolver with the last of his speed loaders. He didn't bother to retrieve the spent holders.

Bob watched to his right and heard men running toward them from the left. He and Cody rose fast and shot into the midst of the group. They remained upright and shot men on the outside of the group before crouching down again.

No gunfire from the right. Cody yelled, "Leo, did you get them all?"

"No way! They're hiding!"

"Same here!" Cody said. "Bob, stay still and cover both of us the best you can."

Bob raised his head and looked both ways. "Hold on, people. Have a look. Our attackers are moving away!"

Cody looked up and saw the backs of two men running hard at an angle from them.

Leo yelled at them. "Smart men!"

Leo wasted four bullets by firing into the air behind them.

Cody saw no more men running. "They're not guards. They're workers! We're not facing dangerous men at all!"

Leo turned back to him. "I like this piece! But as you said, the fighting is unfair. These guys can't shoot! We'll have to defend ourselves if they shoot at us again. Is that what you're saying, Cody?"

"Exactly. I really don't like shooting ducks in a barrel."

Bob said, "Let's not change sides in the middle of the battle, men. We're here on a mission. Let's finish the job. If they come at us, we defend ourselves."

They looked at Bob who aimed and turned his body slightly. He squeezed off his shot at a man aiming his rifle at them. He dropped.

Cody said, "That's the way I taught you to shoot, Bob. Thanks!"

Bob looked down at the rifle's open slide. "I'm out."

Cody and Leo dropped their clips and counted rounds before locking them back in position. He said, "I have four rounds."

Leo said, "Three. Cody, at the first opportunity, you might want to steal three more rifles."

The main house stood in front of them facing the east, meaning they could enter there or at the back door and face the real body guards that had machine guns. Regardless of the guards, he felt the back of the house would be the safest. He looked up at the top floor. The windows could have snipers that could take them out at any time. Fortunately, the entire ranch had not been prepared for the surprise attack. He said, "Those top windows are empty!"

Bob said, "Let's move but hug the terrace with the shrubbery."

They worked their way under the tall shrubs that surrounded ground floor windows. They hesitated near the west end. If they jumped through the windows in their sparse clothing, the glass would butcher them. Their lives still depended upon the cover of the shrubs. "Forget the windows, Cody, Bob said. "Let's find that back door!"

Cody thought about many cavities in the rooms and hallways that could hide shooters. He turned to Leo, while they ran bent over and bouncing off the wall for support. Leo asked while panting heavily, "I don't know about this! Will we actually have better cover in the house, Cody? "

Cody responded. "I hope so! I think all the armed guards are off regrouping or something."

Leo nodded, "I also think we might've also lost our element of surprise."

They met no resistance between them and the back door. Cody remembered the old house. He remembered the telephone by the door in the kitchen at the back door. He burst through the back door and faced one surprised chef. Cody pointed his revolver at the man dressed in starched white clothes and apron. He held his index finger to his lips.

The cook stood frozen and stared at the three men intently. He held a meat cleaver in his right hand but when he saw Cody staring at it, he dropped it and raised both hands.

Cody jerked the wire from the telephone and rushed forward with Bob and Leo at his heels. Leo stopped and gave the chef a last glance before completely leaving him. The man didn't appear to be a threat.

Cody stopped at the first three bedrooms and found them empty. He ran to the offices and found an elderly man sitting at his desk. Two heavily armed men in nylon suits raised their weapons toward and attempted to squeeze the triggers. Both men fell almost at the same time. The older man looked up in surprise and went for the gun he kept in a nearby drawer. He came up with it fast. Not liking what he had to do, Cody shot him through the heart. He man's body jerked back over his leather-backed chair and fell to the floor. His small revolver dropped harmlessly to the side of his swivel chair.

He heard a woman scream. Bob had opened a door to another room. Cody heard two harsh shots. Cody slid to a stop behind Bob, who turned around and looked innocently at him. "No!" Bob answered Copy's anticipated question. "I just shot a man who was pawing a lady. I also shot his buddy if that's okay with you?"

A butler quickly stepped into view before Cody could respond. A maid also entered and screamed. The butler grabbed her and she cut the scream short.

Cody nodded to the butler. He said in Spanish, "Have no fear. We mean you no harm!"

The maid's face remained contorted in pain. The butler, unsmiling, understood and nodded.

"Senor Rubio?" Cody asked.

The butler nodded. *"El joven* (The youngest)." The butler then used his English that he learned in the United States. "He has two sons and an older brother. He also has a lawyer, a most harsh and cruel man. The sons are killers, very dangerous."

Cody gave the man a smile and slapped his shoulder. "Thank you, *Senor!*"

Leo had already moved forward and opened doors, finding no one. The four people stood helplessly and looked at one another. Cody finally broke the silence.

"Looks like the war is small in this house." He said it in English and the Butler replied.

"It will grow big here, *senores!* Be very careful."

The maid, understanding nothing looked up at the butler for any type of explanation. The butler spoke a few words of comfort to her. Bob and Cody had already disappeared to catch up with Leo. The three of them hesitated in the big room where tall, double doors marked the way to the outside. Cody looked outside. Bob and Leo watched behind them before also looking outside.

They spotted several men running for other houses. More than twenty sentries ran for the nearest house east of the big house. Plantation workers without guns dropped what they carried and ran for the trees. A few shabby huts stood closer. Many workers dived into them. Open—air canopies over large vats could be seen in the absence of many sentries.

"Now what?" Leo asked, feeling like they had paused atop a lit powder keg.

Off to their left, Cody spotted the garage where he had once made an escape. Three cars parked close to it appeared empty. Cody thought of an escape plan. The sun beat down on the empty space outside. Everything seemed still but perfect for an ambush. Across a wide clearing stood the house where they thought most of the sentries could be hiding and not regrouping with a plan.

"It appears they fled into that house. That may be where more big bosses are located," Cody suggested.

Leo chuckled. "The owners are probably not in a very good mood right now with most of his soldiers hiding under his feet. Let's not give them time to plan any new battles."

"Those hired soldiers are nothing but untrained laborers." Bob said with regret. "Some of them will be fighters. How do we distinguish them from the workers?"

"Bob asked a sensible question for once." Leo said. "But we just can't walk up to the front porch and ask them to go home."

They heard loud voices from the nearest door and Cody spotted two men with rifles creep toward the front door of the big house. Neither man got a shot off but both dropped from Cody's rifle. Leo scrambled outside and recovered the rifles without drawing fire.

Cody nodded to Leo and said, "That was dumb."

Leo, already saddened, said, "No. It wasn't. These other guys don't want to kill us. They're scared!"

Cody agreed. "Well, take heart. There are plenty remaining that ain't scared. The fighters among them are probably forcing the workers to fight. We have to deal with those guys."

Bob snatched one rifle and scrambled back behind a couch.

"Better count your ammo, Bob!" Cody growled and began unloading the other rifle to see how far they could take the next fight.

Someone rang the doorbell and the butler rushed to pause before Cody, who used Spanish. "Careful, friend!"

At that time a well—dressed man appeared from behind a curtain to stand close to a large safe. He lifted his gun at Cody's back but Bob lifted his gun first and shot the man in the center of his chest. Cody saw this from the corner of his eye and looked at Bob, who merely shrugged.

Leo asked Bob, "Are you having fun? That man was about to take Cody off probation."

The butler grimaced from the noise and quickly gained control. He nodded to Leo and proceeded forward very unsure of himself. The maid clung to him. He opened the door and the two men, well-armed and standing on the outside, asked if the three invaders were inside the house.

The butler answered in a large voice. "Of course! They have no quarrel with me or any of my staff."

They nodded to one another and quietly whispered that they would wait for more men. They did not want to fight.

More workers stepped out to call to Cody and his two friends. Cody showed himself in the doorway and said, "I have words for you and all the men here."

The spokesman, not one of the workers, Cody imagined, drew a deep breath and talked loud enough for everyone to hear. "Speak your words, *gringo,* and explain why you have attacked us!"

"Call the others out where everyone can hear me!" Cody half-yelled to him.

The spokesman said, "You have killed our men! They were only poor laborers. Why are you doing this?"

Cody yelled at the man. Many men dodged backward at the sound of his voice. "Do not be a liar! We only kill men who are trying to kill us!"

Several men stepped outside and joined those huddled behind the spokesman. Cody caught a new breath of air and spoke in his best Spanish. "We have killed many men today. We came here to destroy this place! If you try to stop us, you will be killed. Men, go home and leave all your arms on the ground right where you are standing. Go in peace--leave here!--or you can remain and fight!"

The spokesman, still attempting to be brave, asked, "How do we know you will not shoot us?"

Cody shook his head sadly. "If we desired to kill you, you would already be dead! Go!"

Leo spoke up. "Nice going, Cody. Did you tell them that we are going to give up?"

The men muttered as they dropped their rifles and turned toward the small shacks a short distance south. Lastly, the spokesman dropped his rifle and glared at Cody.

Cody turned his head slightly toward Leo. "Not to worry about Bob and me, Leo. I told them that you were the only one who shot them."

The spokesman shouted to the workers. Go to your homes! These men will not kill you. Hurry!"

Cody placed his empty revolver behind him and grinned at the man. "I wish we had talked earlier."

The man stepped around his rifle and followed the others.

They rearranged chairs in the living room and settled where they could see the door and windows. After a few moments of silence inside and out, the butler rushed inside the room toward Cody with fear in his voice. He tried to be calm but failed.

"You must leave, sir. Either leave or give yourselves up. There are at least 40 men who are the bodyguards in this house who have been hiding with their machine guns. They wanted the workers to kill you. Now, they are meeting together to kill all three of you."

Cody had wondered where they were but he knew that he would know soon enough. He motioned for Leo and Bob to follow him toward the garage. On their way they gathered up all the rifles they could carry. He turned back to the butler and nodded his thanks.

"Okay, Cody," Leo said. "What's up?"

Cody explained. The house's main guards number about forty. They are inside the house as we speak. They are the professionals. What's changed is that we are going to be holed up in the garage or in the brush. Let's fight from the windows."

They gathered all the rifles they could find from the other house. Once they had all they could hold in their arms, they huddled inside the garage.

Cody said, "We had better collect the ammo, guys. We may be in for a real fight!"

CHAPTER 22

They had just positioned themselves by three windows of the garage when a new group of men approached with weapons and dropped them on the ground. Most of them kept their hands in the air.

Cody yelled through the glass and told them to go home. He guessed them to be at least fifty in number.

Their leader outside seemed at ease and didn't move. Cody called to him as he walked a few steps toward the window. "Gather all the rifles you can carry and toss them through the door here."

Cody asked Leo and Bob to find cover fast. The blinds at one window had moved slightly in the big house. Bob fired first and the blind fell in pieces as if torn down by a falling body.

Cody dodged from the wall as machine gun bullets passed through the wooden walls and ricocheted off the floor. The last man talking to Cody toppled forward in the doorway, dead from the bullets that caught him in the back and front.

Cody and his partners found protection on the opposite side of a large sedan. He hugged the car with his back and watched as Leo and Bob fired into the wall of the house and demolished the blinds that had covered the window of the large house in the forward area.

"That's showing 'em, guys!" he said loudly to Leo and Bob.

"Thanks, boss!" Leo said. "Feel free to join us."

Cody fired a short burst from the window and crawled rapidly back to the safety of the car. "This is not a good place to fight."

They made their way around the garage to the back door. One man from the outside jumped free of the door. He jumped high and turned in mid-air to fire at Cody but caught a bullet in his chest. He back awkwardly, dead.

Cody thought he heard footsteps behind him but wasn't sure due to being deafened by noise. He turned in time to see Bob flying toward him and stopped.

Bob held his automatic in front of him and dug in his pocket for another clip. Cody did the same.

"We have to take that house!" Bob said, his voice raised to overcome their deafness.

"No other choice!" Cody yelled. "Let's hold each door we cover until they rush us from other entrances. Then we have to fight whoever is in sight."

Bob nodded and motioned for Leo to follow as they dove inside and slid across the large floor. The bodies of three well-dressed men lay still on the floor. They had occupied windows of the large room.

Cody found the hallway and began shooting into a large crowd of well-dressed men. They huddled with guns hardly fifty feet distant. He felt they had done well by attacking the professional bodyguards instead of waiting to be attacked. The mass of men reversed direction and ran over men behind them. Cody kept firing as men fell. Bullets slammed into the door sidings on each side of him. The shooters scrambled out of sight. Cody reached a door with his partners trailing closely.

He shot as fast as he could with a rifle and quickly ran out of bullets. He picked up another to resume fire. All the professionals disappeared. At least twenty men lay dead or bleeding in the hallway. They seemed well-dressed enough to meet their maker.

Both Leo and Bob had also fired and stopped. Most of them, they surmised, had taken doors bordering the long hallway.

Cody left in the direction of Bob and Leo. No one occupied either of the first two doors he opened. The bullets had ceased from the outside. He carried only one rifle and dropped the clip to check the live rounds. He had four rounds remaining from what he guessed was a thirty-round clip.

Cody yelled at Leo. "No one left here! Let's..."

Bob fired as a man leaped from a closet, who dropped to the floor with a large machine gun in his hands.

Cody fired blindly into the closet in the other room. He heard nothing from behind the door.

Leo called, "What did you say?"

Cody said, "This house is not secure. I'm going to pick up a couple of those automatic rifles. Don't shoot me!"

"Just hold your ID in front of you so I can see it, Cody!" Leo yelled back. "They're going to rush me from behind if I don't move!"

Bob ran straight to Leo. "We're coming!"

Cody stopped and snatched a rifle. He pulled the magazine from another just like it and hoped it was full. "Look, guys, let's not bust through each door to dig those guys out. Let's get back to the garage where I'll feel a great deal safer for Leo. There was a gas barrel in there. We may have better luck burning these guys out."

Bob disagreed. "Forget that! A cautionary war can last for weeks. Let's continue to bust through the doors and get it over with. Two at a time, you see, one shoots from the waist and one shoots low from the floor."

Cody agreed. "All right! Suicide it is! Give me a two-minute head start so I can run outside through the brush like a wild cow."

Leo surprised Cody by laughing at another man's joke. Bob even grinned. Leo said, "No way, Cody. You're still on probation. You get to shoot from the floor under Bob's rifle. I'll be running ahead in alert status and knocking on doors to warn them you're coming."

Cody agreed and Bob shook his head sadly at such ridiculous humor. He paused short of one door and shot several times through it before kicking it open. They met bullets as Bob kept firing and Cody dropped to the floor between Bob's feet. He managed to shoot one man who was already falling, along with two others.

Cody looked ahead and saw Leo doing the same thing. He snatched Bob's right arm and pulled himself up. "This ain't working, Bob. I'm doing the next one solo. You'd best go back and find a rifle with more ammo in it."

Bob said, "Good idea. But first check the closets in this room. Cody pointed his rifle as two started firing through the closet door. Bob cringed and Cody shot one in the open and the other through the door. He turned back to Bob.

"Why did you jump?"

Bob showed him his arm. "I'm afraid that I caught one."

Cody shouted at Leo to hold up due to a medical emergency.

Leo shouted back. "I knew that I should not have let you two work alone! How serious?"

"Bob has a flesh wound in his upper muscle in his left arm. I'm going to have to tie it off."

"Use a bedsheet!" Leo grumbled loudly.

Cody was thinking why a bedsheet when it struck him to rip it into long bandages. He snatched a sheet and wrestled it away from the other coverings.

Bob helped him hold the sheet and furnished a knife to start the ripping. In no time Cody had ripped Bob's shirt sleeve and checked for a broken bone. Bob cringed once and straightened. Cody wrapped the wound then decided to look at it. He saw where a bullet did graze his arm but barely deep enough to bring blood to the surface. He tossed the ripped bandages aside and pushed Bob out the door. "Jeeze, Bob. We'll have to fly you to a hospital. You're losing blood too fast to save you."

Bob decided to look at the wound, himself, and said, "Well, it hurt bad enough to be serious." He took off toward Leo while holding a rifle in his free hand. "I'd fare better with a side arm instead of a rifle."

Cody said, "Sorry, old buddy. I am out of ammo for side arms. If I find any nine millimeters I'll load it for you."

Bob spoke dryly. "Try a ten millimeter. Nine is for women."

Leo shot steadily into the side rooms. When he stopped a moment later, he lifted a rifle from a dead man and said, "I'll cover you if you want to try for the garage again!"

Cody ran for the garage and lifted the door. He found one man crouching behind the trunk of a huge luxury sedan. Cody called to him. *"Oye, compadre! Da me los llaves por el carro!* (Listen, pal, give me the keys to the car!")

The man stood up and presented Cody a key. He nodded toward the house. He said in English, "It is the car of *Senor* Rubio!"

Cody also used English. "We are going to Bogota. Do you want a ride with us?"

"No. I am paid to take care of things here, including this very nice car!"

Cody nodded. "Suit yourself. Is there petrol here?"

The man pointed to several five-gallon cans. "The petrol is for the truck!"

Again, Cody agreed. "I am borrowing two cans. Seat yourself and wait. There may be more shooting."

"Did you shoot many people, sir?"

"Not many! Have yourself a good day!"

Cody moved to the pile of guns and began to pour gasoline over them. He gave the half-full can to Leo and said, "Burn that back entrance and the entire house. Aw heck! Take this other can, too. Burn this sucker to the ground! I'll get more gas from the garage."

After running across the yard again, Cody had to lift the garage door again. The care keeper still hid behind the trunk.

Curious, Cody walked to the rear of the car. There, sitting scared and holding a young woman held a frightened man in her arms. She seemed to have more control than her man.

Cody smiled at her and told the man squatting next to her to have no fear. "Give me no problems, understand?"

The man nodded his approval and Cody said, "I need two more cans of petrol."

"Okay!" the man said.

Cody took his time. All the guards, apparently, had no weapons and saw no further reason for war. He poured gasoline inside the foreman's house and stepped back. He had no matches. He called to Leo and Bob. "Do you guys have matches?"

Leo yelled back. "I found some in the kitchen. Bob came running at full speed. "Cody, you should never give gasoline to an Irishman!

Cody looked at questionably. "Why?"

A loud "Whoosh!" sounded from the inside followed by flames that reached their position and set the guns afire. Cody stepped back with the cans of gasoline. Leo came through the flames that had died down. He yelled, "Yee-haw! Man, this Colombian gas is some kind of volatile!"

The sudden fire had singed Leo's eyebrows and hair at the back of his head. His charred face proved a flash fire had beaten him.

Cody poured gas inside on the walls and floor. He held a cautionary hand in front of Leo. "Wait until I'm clear then toss the match! You don't need to stand over the gas and hold your hand over the match's flame to shield it from the wind!"

None of the masses showed themselves on their side of the house. A few still armed hurried around one corner. Bob shot them as rapidly as they appeared.

Bob followed Cody and helped him set the pits on fire. He poured it over many kilos of bundles, also. They found no unpackaged cocaine. The new owner would have had few problems getting the place back in business. He burned everything akin to cocaine manufacturing.

"I have the keys to a car that will take us back to town if Leo hasn't set himself on fire again."

Leo met them at the garage door. "Guys, do we have ourselves an easy job or what?"

Bob said, "Don't be arrogant, Leo."

Cody drove the almost new luxury car to the middle of the compound. They looked at the weathered shacks and spotted dark figures in the windows. They would be out of work, now. Cody suddenly beamed with a new thought!

He left the car and walked toward the shacks. Follow me, gents. I am working on an idea. They fell in behind him.

Leo mumbled, "You might be getting us mobbed with your idea, Cody. Usually your ideas cost Bob and me about ten years of our lives when you suddenly think that you can land an airplane in a crowded parking lot or something."

Cody opened the door of the first shack. He spoke in the Spanish language. Several women, mostly elderly, watched him fearfully. "Listen to me, all of you! Your big boss is dead. The chief no longer lives. We mean you no harm. We are not at war with you poor people! Come out of the houses. I have good news for all of you!"

They all stood still, not trusting the foreigners who just burned their livelihood and killed many of their men. Cody backed up and motioned for them to come. A few followed.

He said, "Look, if I wanted to bring problems to you, your little houses would not stop me. I would burn them all with you inside. I am serious! Follow me! Come! Bring the children and grandfathers! Hurry!"

Bob said, "Hide your face, Leo. I think you're scaring the children!"

"Stuff it, Bob! If you want to talk, tell me what Cody is up to."

"I have no idea! He wants them outside. I think they think he's going to shoot all of them."

It required another five minutes for all the people to slowly leave their shelters.

He explained again that if he wanted to kill them or give them problems, he would burn their homes with them inside again. They frowned and ambled toward him.

When they surrounded him curiously, he explained. "Listen, we are not your enemies! Inside the house is a vault. It contains a much money. Wait until the fire is out and break the locks on the vault. Take the money and divide it equally!"

"Tomorrow, or sooner, the army will come. They will take the money and they will not share it with you. It is your money! Take it and leave this place!"

"Will the police come for us?" one of them asked

"Yes! They will also take your money if they catch you! Open that vault and divide the money, but you must flee from here! Run before the police arrive! Go far! Run through the trees and live in the trees until you feel safe. No! Not now! Get the money first!"

Many of them came forward to shake his hand. Many of the women hugged him. Many of the older men did the same. They asked God to bless him and his friends. They hugged Leo and Bob, also.

Leo said, "I'm outta here! This hero stuff ain't for me."

Cody and Bob followed him. Bob nudged Cody with his elbow. "I heard you mention money. I am assuming you're talking about the huge safe in that man's office that you deliberately shot and killed in cold blood."

Cody nodded and grunted affirmatively.

"These people have no tools. How do you expect them to open it?"

"Bob, look around you. Let me tell you something about the people who live in our hemisphere. They not only thrive in harsh conditions of disease and poverty, they are the most prolific, fruitful or productive people in the world. India and China have nothing on them. The Muslims think they will control the world in only a few decades. Wrong!"

"Oh—great!" Bob scoffed. "Now you're an anthropologist!"

"What I'm saying is this: Take away their tools and they will make their own. Take their resources and they become resourceful."

"They'll find hammers and that big safe will be a crushed beer can by nightfall."

Bob had enough. Cody had a long, overdue lecture. A disturbance behind them snatched their attention.

CHAPTER 23

They turned to see four or five young women coming for them with two men attempting to hold them back.

"Help us!" they cried out in English to Cody and his partners. They jerked their arms free of the men attempting to hold them.

The men holding on the younger ladies stopped and ran when the three dangerous foreigners spun to face them. The girls came forward, five of them, all talking at once and in perfect English. "Please help us!"

Leo spoke first. He saw their bare feet and sack dresses but they wore lipstick and eye makeup while the other women wore no makeup. "Hellooo! What have we here?"

"We're United States citizens and we are here against our will. We are prisoners!" one of them said.

"We were kidnapped on our way home from school! We don't want to be here! Help us, please!"

Cody held both hands up. "Whoa! Hold on, one at a time. What do you mean by not wanting to be here?"

"We were kidnapped!" another said. We were walking home from school and these men jumped from a van and brought a bunch of us here and to other ranches."

"When?" Bob asked, feeling alarmed and eyeing the men watching at a distance.

"Over a year ago. There were more. They got pregnant and disappeared. The women make us work in the house either cooking or cleaning house all day. We were in high school when they abducted us."

"Well, for goodness sake!" Bob exclaimed. Where is your home? Where are your parents?"

"We were kidnapped in Los Angeles, California. More than fifty of us were kidnapped that one day! We were all taken off the school grounds while our teachers watched helplessly!"

"Your English is good!" Leo said.

"So is your English!" one said. "We hardly knew any Spanish until we came here. We had to learn or else the old women beat us with broom handles!"

Cody asked no one in particular, "What were those men holding you back from us for?"

"To keep us away from you guys! They're all married to the old women but they want us just like the younger men want us. They were the ones that guarded this place."

Cody couldn't believe what he heard. "Perhaps we better have a talk with these men."

"Talk all you want." One said. "It will mean nothing to them. They are cruel to us and their wives."

Leo turned to Cody, "Well, it looks like you've done it again, Cody. You crashed and burned but this time is a little different."

Cody looked back at the luxury sedan. "Do you think eight of us can ride in that thing?"

The girls all said, "Yes" at the same time.

"Then let's move out before help arrives. The smoke can be seen over the mountains between here and Bogota, I'm sure."

Cody tossed the keys to Bob. "Get 'em to a U. S. Embassy. Probably one in Bogota, possibly."

"What's up, Cody?" Leo asked. Are you taking me with you somewhere else?"

"No. We're following Bob to Bogota in whatever vehicle we can muster."

"Why can't we stay with Bob and the girls?"

"Because we cannot get them back to safety crowded up in that car!" Cody replied equally as anxious. "What if we had to shoot from that car with those girls inside?"

Leo looked at the house. "Perhaps we should stick around and wait for the army to arrive."

Cody looked at Bob, who nodded his agreement. Cody walked back into the garage and this time he told the caretaker that he wanted to borrow the acetylene torch and bottles. Everyone waited.

When darkness finally engulfed them hours later, Cody moved his cutting torch passed many glowing embers. He felt the heat embrace his face as he adjusted the flame and began his work.

One of the workers stood by with a sledge hammer and knocked away the cement in order for Cody to cut the lever. When he opened the safe, several people moved in. Cody stepped back. The man with the hammer touched his arm and asked him to remove the money.

With a man's flashlight, he leaned inside and found a large stack of new bills from the bank. After removing more paper and bonds, he found two more large bundles of money. He carried all three stacks in front of the headlights. Including the guards, he counted 163 people. He looked at the girls and changed the number to 168. Then he counted the money.

There appeared to be 200,000 in each stack, packaged neatly in plastic bindings and paper.

Leo rapidly computed how many dollars they had and how much each individual could claim.

Leo looked away into the crowd of people all waiting patiently, then back to Cody. Pass out $3,592 each. There will be change remaining. Leave it for the army.

Cody chuckled. The whole crowd joined in. He said, "That's going to be a little tricky. All we have are hundreds and fifties."

Leo said, "Let them figure it out. Take $14,365 to the girls and tell them to divvy it up. It's their cut."

"Now announce to the crowd how much each one has coming, assuming your count of 168 was correct."

Cody did that and pointed to the man with the sledge hammer would be passing out the money. It would be difficult due to having all bills the size of hundreds and fifties. They all whistled and applauded Cody. The man with the sledge also grinned and applauded. Cody spoke to the man where most people could hear him. Be fair and honest with the people. Like you, they are out of work.

The guards protested, claiming they had more money coming. Cody told them to be silent, that they were getting a bonus to their wages.

Cody drove a sedan with Leo riding shotgun. Bob pulled in behind them as they left the ranch.

Leo said, "That's one down with one more to go."

One of the girls in the back seat of Bob's car, said, "Man, you guys can really fight! Who are you?"

Bob shrugged, "Just some officers doing their jobs."

She said, "I know the story of one man who came to this very ranch one time. An old woman told it to me early one morning when we talked of us escaping this terrible prison for us. She told me the owners had tigers that they would feed with people who were bad on the ranch or some man who was too lazy to work. She said they went to America once and stole a white woman from her home. They treated her bad. They one day her husband came like a ghost! She said that he had no car or horse. He just appeared out of nowhere and began shooting people who worked for the owners. She said he walked inside the big house right out of the night and shot man after man. Sometimes several of them shot at him and he killed them all. When he found his wife, he killed more guards and walked her across the big yard and they both vanished."

Bob laughed, "You don't want to believe all that you hear. There are good people who will fight for you but they are not invincible and they are not ghosts. Such tales grow too large. Do not believe them."

But you three men came out of nowhere and beat all of the guards!"

"We are good with weapons. Your guards were not good. If they were good with weapons, all three of us would be dead."

She sat back. "But this man she told me about was a ghost."

Bob grinned. "He is not a ghost. He is that man driving the car in front of us. Do not believe stories like that. Just believe that he will fight for truth and justice."

They traveled the dirt road until it connected to the highway leading into Bogota. A group of men appearing to be soldiers appeared to be expecting them. They men stood in a large circle that allowed them to surround everyone in the both cars. They had flashlights that blinded both Cody and Leo. One pickup had a large portable light that held fast to the car following Cody. Bob and the girls stood no chance of escaping. The girls quickly folded their bills and passed them to Bob, who shoved them inside his shorts in the crotch area.

"Are they soldiers?" Cody asked.

"I fear not." Leo replied almost lifeless.

Bob also felt his stomach turmoil as all doors flew open, filling their space with light the same time someone grasped their arms and rudely jerked them from the vehicle. Everyone, including Bob, sprawled flat on the rough pavement.

Neither Cody nor Leo resisted as they flew sideways onto the unforgiving asphalt. They both received blows that slammed them back on the pavement once they attempted to sit.

"Do you wish to anger us? You are only one little man. But be careful. If you anger us, we will stop and kill one or two of your precious young women!"

"Of course you will! How much money do your bosses pay this Russian?"

"I don't know if the Russian will be paid or not. He said that he would eliminate all three of you free of money. But we will send Moscow a large shipment of cocaine to show our appreciation."

"You could pay me to kill the Russian and save your shipment of cocaine."

This brought a chuckle from the driver. You will have your chance to prove yourselves against this Russian."

"What if I defeat this Russian in a fair fight? Will you still kill us?"

"Yes. You will die from bullets. We will shoot your legs and feet. We will chop off your arms with machetes. You will die slowly."

Leo laughed again. "Please stop. You are making me very scared and such thoughts will disturb my sleep. Let these young women go! They have done you no harm."

"They will provide us entertainment. We like them. They will have our babies. When they grow older, we will kill them."

"Nice folks." Leo said. "You realize that you are an embarrassment to the human race."

The driver interpreted what he said and laughed with his partner.

CHAPTER 24

Cody guessed they traveled twenty miles west before slowing and turning off the narrow pavement. The forest cries had already begun shortly after darkness swept over the land. They traveled through large trees huddled thick with three levels of growth all connecting together. The limbs over the narrow road connected above the cabs with limbs from the other side of the road, giving them a sense of entering into a dark cave. As soon as the forest cleared he spotted the lights of the ranch. The dark mountains seemed to have widened, and he knew such farms would extend for miles within the valley.

The vehicles pulled into the huge yard in front of the main house. From the overhead lights of the vehicles and outside lights from the buildings, Cody guessed at least 200 people closed in to get a glimpse of the three men who burned the large ranch and killed many people.

Cody caught a glimpse of Leo for an instant. Guns pointed at his head and body while he walked straight into the crowd. He looked to his side among his guards and spotted Bob, also well-guarded. He spoke in Italian.

"Men, make your escape while I keep the people busy."

"No—Leo! Wait..."

The punches Cody received for talking caused all sounds from Leo to deafen. He said nothing in reply.

Bob apparently replied. The punches he received caused his knees to buckle. Cody yelled in Spanish, "Hey—hey! Wait—wait! We are not attempting to escape...!

That's when he heard Leo's voice far louder than the crowd's. "Hey! Where is your champion? Where is the Russian? I want to see this big man who claims he can beat me!"

He said this in English. Cody quickly translated for his guards, also heard by Bob's protests. Enough people understood Leo. They grew quieter. Only a few mutterings among the crowd could be heard in the stillness.

Then a loud voice boomed from the big house. He also spoke in English, although broken. "I am here, American dog!"

Leo yelled to him. "Come! Show me how you will tear my arms from my body!"

One of the guards quickly translated. The crowd closed around Leo.

The cartel's attorney seized Sasha Kroschov's arm. "Do not fall for this trick, Sasha! The American is up to something."

Sasha broke free of the lawyer's grasp and yelled, "We will not fight tonight! We will wait until tomorrow when we will have a ring and many visitors see you suffer!"

The crowd grew excited. The guards attempted to push Cody and Bob forward. Cody said in English, "Wait! There is no fight tonight. But look, we want to show you a trick."

Leo's voice sounded above the noise again. "Move out of my way! Give me room to kill the dirty Russian with my hands tied behind my back!"

Sasha jumped into the crowd and threw men aside. "Move! I will give you a taste of what I will do to this American tomorrow!"

The crowd made a large ring, even though many spectators shoved from behind. Cody's guards looked forward anxiously. He glanced at Bob, who, within a second, jumped high enough to bring his knees and boots up, sufficiently high enough to allow his feet and legs pass above his handcuffed hands. After landing on his feet, his handcuffed hands held proudly in front of him.

Cody protested. "I was supposed to do that first, Bob!" While he said it, he did exactly the same thing. Men watching muttered that they could do that and began jumping above their clasped hands.

Cody said, "See? Watch this!" In spite of the guns pointing toward him, he jumped again. With his hands in front of him, he quickly disarmed the nearest guard shortly before kicking him in the forehead with his right knee.

That guard went down and Cody shoved the butt of his rile into the face of another guard who turned to see what happened. Bob did exactly the same thing to his nearest guard only he kicked the man in the face with his farthest foot. Then he snatched the rifle soundlessly in time to swing the butt into the face of the other guard that turned around to see the scuffling behind him.

While everyone crowded to see the Russian kill the American with his bare hands, Cody and Bob ran as fast as possible to the nearest pickup. The keys hung in the ignition. Bob jumped the hood and swung back to open the passenger door. Cody had the engine running and in gear by the time Bob slammed his door.

The lawyer, who stood on the steps well above the crowd screamed at the people watching Leo and the Russian. "They are escaping! Get them! Hurry!"

Leo kept yelling at the Russian who came at him like a charging rhinoceros. He thought, "Cody, I hope you and Bob make your move now! I am giving up my life to save you guys!"

Once underway, Bob opened his belt buckle. "I don't suppose you thought to bring a handcuff key!"

Embarrassed, Cody said, "I didn't plan on getting captured, Bob! Okay, you got me! I forgot it."

After freeing his hands with the key he always carried in his belt, Bob leaned over and unlocked Cody's cuffs.

While the lawyer jumped and screamed from his position on the steps, Leo jumped far into the air and slipped his knees and feet between his arms. As his feet touched the ground he jumped again and extended both feet toward the charging man's face. Both feet found his chest solidly. Leo dropped to the parking lot on his shoulders but his handcuffed hands in front braced his fall. He didn't feel the impact with his feet as well as he wanted. He knew he failed to hurt the Russian when the big man jumped and landed on Leo's chest with his wide bottom.

"This is it!" Leo thought. "My chest is surely crushed against my heart and lungs! Run, Cody and Bob! May God bless the both of you!" He thought he only imagined these words but soon realized that he yelled them.

Sasha Kroschev heard the lawyer's words and stopped, looked back at him and wondered how comical he appeared, jumping up and down, pointing and yelling.

Leo kept silent as he thought his next words. "I am alive. I hurt but I am alive!"

Cody and Bob raced away from the compound. No one followed, yet.

Cody had the accelerator pressed to the floor. He needed to out distance his pursuers once they came to their senses.

Bob yelled, "No lights behind us! Slow down!"

Cody slowed. "Get ready to bail!"

They both opened their doors as the first headlights closed in on the road behind them. They jumped high and turned in the air to allow their feet to touch the earth first. They expected to be able to slide to a stop but their momentum proved too great. They tumbled into the trees and both struck the unforgiving trunks before their momentum ended abruptly. Cody's breath left him temporarily.

Bob grunted when he contacted a tree. "Are you okay, Cody?"

"Yeah! Let's move!"

The headlights of the first pickup roared passed them, gaining on the slow pickup ahead. Two men stood in the bed of the truck. The second truck whipped by them in a rush. Two more men with rifles occupied the bed. They prepared to ambush the third and final truck.

The first two trucks slowed and braked as the escape vehicle crashed into a tree within two feet of leaving the road. The third pick up passed them at a much slower speed.

Cody jumped for the bed feet first and thought he saw Bob do the same thing. Both armed men didn't see what hit them at waist level. They bumped into one another and fell backward. Cody and Bob, moving as fast as possible, snatched the AR-47's and threw them off safety. Cody turned toward the left side of the cab and shot through it, catching the driver dead center. Bob, slower by a fraction of a second, fired and the passenger lunged forward with a bullet through his back.

The truck plowed into thick brush off the road and stopped. Both Cody and Bob opened the doors and fished two more rifles from the cab of the small truck. The two guards in the back stood up in the road with raised hands.

Cody struck the nearest man as hard as he could in the face with the butt of his rifle. Bob did the same. Both men would be out of the war for days.

The two vehicles ahead of them turned around.

Cody said, "I got the headlights of both vehicles. You get the two men standing behind the cab."

"Roger that!" Bob replied and aimed above the cab of the nearest truck to see a dark outline of a man. Then it suddenly turned dark as the headlights disappeared from Cody's two shots, almost simultaneously.

The truck pulled to one side and Cody shot the headlamps of the other truck. He aimed for the nearest driver but failed to see him. He shot several times through the cab and windshield of both vehicles. Bob did the same.

Cody said, "Let's assess the damage to the men up there and gather some more ammo. We're going to run short if we attack that ranch."

They found seven dead men and one wounded. "Shot through the shoulder," Bob said.

"One of your bullets," Cody said jokingly.

Bob agreed. "If I remember correctly, I was the only one doing any shooting!"

"Atta boy, Leo!" Cody said almost chuckling. "Good job! He's out of the fight."

They kept all the magazines they could find. Some of them packed full and others felt lighter. Cody took the time to fill all the clips with what cartridges they could find.

Leo, on the other hand, felt his sprained ribs and attempted to get up to watch the ruckus. Sasha saw him from the corner of his eye and backhanded him. Leo felt the back of his head strike the paved ground. He thought, "Me and this guy need to have a serious meeting about sucker punches!"

The crowd applauded Sasha and hissed at Leo. Leo lay where he dropped and waited. Sure enough, Sasha reached down and got a handful of shirt and chest hairs. He smiled at Leo. "Excuse me, please, but I say you are one stupid American, savage pig!"

Leo slowly readied his right hand while still handcuffed to his left. He lied. "I—I don't want trouble with you, sir."

Sasha grinned wider and held his face a little closer to Leo's. "You don't..."

Leo's right fist caught him squarely in the nose with all the power he could muster. He felt his fist strike solid and heavy, and he automatically followed through as if the man's face had never been there. His left hand, still clasped to his right only added to the power. It proved to be a nice punch.

Sasha's voice stopped as his whole body straightened and fell backward with his feet in the air. The crowd fell silent as Leo inspected him, *totally unconscious*. Not even a whisper arose among them. That's when the lawyer made himself heard again.

"They are escaping! Hurry! Two men in front, two in the back! Take your rifles and bring the Americans back alive, if you can!"

The lawyer then pointed to Leo. "Fools! This man is dangerous! Seize him!"

A few men hesitated in front of Leo. None wanted a physical confrontation without sufficient help. Several men jumped on his back while Leo's knees slowly buckled to the ground. They pelted him with fists and shoes to his ribs and back. They kicked his legs and attempted to stamp his hands, which he closed and held them underneath his body. He felt them stand on his neck and head.

"No—no—no!" the lawyer yelled. "Hold him! Bind him with rope! Hurry before he kills all of you!"

Ropes magically appeared as they choked him and bound his arms close to his body. He filled his lungs with air and attempted to save himself slack later. He felt the ropes burn and cut into his arms. They jerked him off his feet and bound his legs together. He felt himself in a cocoon of ropes.

They dragged him around the unconscious Russian and inside one of the buildings. The lawyer encouraged them. "Yes! That is the way! Secure him safely to the large bed. One of you stay with him throughout the night! Do not leave him! Do you understand me? This man is dangerous! We do not want him to escape. Tomorrow, the Russian will tear his arms off his body. You can watch!"

CHAPTER 25

Cody and Bob walked into brush to be even with the helpless vehicles and waited for daylight outside the compound. After waiting several minutes, they walked back and around the two men they struck in the face with rifle butts. Both of them lay in the middle of the road groaning.

They found a hiding place in the brush close to the headquarters. They placed the rifles against a tree with butts down. Cody pointed to a large tree but Bob refused to look.

"I'm not spending another night in the brush, Cody. You can kill time out here all you want but I'm going to rescue Leo and beat feet back to town."

Cody said, "It's an art, Bob. You cannot learn to sleep in a tree if you do not try! Now stop your foolishness and climb a tree until sunup."

Cody managed to reach a limb twice the size of his body or more and stretched out on it.

Bob watched him and punched his leg. "Yo--Cody! Are you asleep yet?"

"Just about. Why?"

"Just checking."

"Bob, I'm tired. Knock off the Leo jokes and stretch out on the limb you just passed. It's big enough. Sleep on your tummy and cross your legs to balance if you tend to roll about. The limb grows upward. You don't need a pillow!"

There are ants on this limb!"

"Okay, find another one!"

"There are monkeys above us in this tree. I can hear them."

"Button your shirt pockets."

"Will they bite?

"Yes. But you have to stick your fingers in their mouths first."

"What if they pee on us?"

"That's why we sleep on our tummies."

"They can poop on us, too!"

"Bob, shut up or go find another tree!"

"I'm going to find another limb higher up."

"Fine! You don't need to call home about it. Don't get too high. The limbs will be smaller. The monkeys will be disturbed and a big cat will climb this tree to see what the fuss is about."

"Baloney!"

Cody didn't reply until several seconds later. "I wonder if Leo is still alive."

"Hush, Cody, I'm trying to sleep!"

Leo chuckled to himself as if someone had told a joke. They had retied each of his wrists tightly to bedposts, stretching his arms as if they might be rubber. He sat on the floor at the foot of a bed. He lifted his knees and stretched one foot above his head and pressed the bottom of his shoe against one bedpost.

"Now, this, Leo," he muttered to himself. "This is what we might call slightly uncomfortable."

The guard approached him and asked what was happening. Although above him and distant, Leo kicked with his right foot and caught the man directly in the face. He fell backward unconscious.

He grunted and struggled to get the other foot against the other bedpost. He planned to push them apart. Being tied fast and hard to each post killed that idea. "Rats!" he swore aloud. He laughed again at his predicament. "Never move on your first idea, Leo!"

He stretched one foot to the bottom of one bedpost and raised his body until he could put the other foot at the bottom of the other post. Then he pushed. Like all wooden furniture, he noted, it hardly gave to the pressure more than a creak. He placed his feet on the floor in front of him and rested.

The second time he tried it he made it creak louder and he felt it give slightly. He rested. The third time he tried it, he felt it splinter. He stopped laughing and gathered all his strength to pull the tops of the bed posts together. The bed posts cooperated. He quickly untangled his ropes and grasped a loose bed post. With that he rendered the guard further into unconsciousness.

He realized that he must sleep lightly as he stretched out on the mattress. He remained clothed. His captors would be displeased the following morning. He yawned and forced himself to think of nothing but sleep. He first muttered to himself. "I wonder if Cody and Bob are still alive."

He lay there for an hour. He attempted to sleep but his mind remained clouded by "What if's?" He tried a window. Too tight. He knocked on the door to wake a guard. No answer. He looked at the ceiling and saw rafters. His wall only went seven feet high before it stopped without a ceiling. Many well placed rafters above him held the roof steady. He stood on the back bed post and boosted himself up and over the wall. He failed to reach the rafters by two feet.

The sun beat down on Cody and Bob before they could become fully awake. It had been a short nap. Bob climbed noisily down. Cody awakened but didn't move. He knew where he was and recognized Bob's movements.

Bob looked up and said, "Good morning, Cody. Did you sleep well?"

"I did. How about yourself?"

"Lousy, thank you!"

"Did you sleep at all Bob?"

"Yes, for about ten minutes. I've never been so scared of falling out of bed."

Cody stretched before he moved. "Not a problem, then. All you needed was a little sleep. Our bodies can take the punishment for a few days but our minds need to sleep a little."

"I appreciate the concept, Cody. I'm sleeping on the ground next time."

"Not a good idea, Bob. If the ants, scorpions, centipedes, ticks, cockroaches and snakes don't kill you, a jaguar or some other species of a wild cat will."

"That's all theory, Junior."

"Perhaps," Cody replied, "but it keeps me in the trees."

"Do you have a theory about rescuing Leo and burning this place to the ground?"

"Yes. We wait here by the road and wait until they miss their twelve people. We'll take them out by numbers."

"Among your brilliant ideas, partner, remember that we need food and water. I haven't had any coffee!"

Cody ignored him. Bob liked to pass the time lightly when Leo wasn't present. "We'll wait after sunrise tomorrow if you want, Bob. Personally, I'm tired. There's only one way in and out of that place, anyway."

Bob sat down and braced his back on the nearest tree trunk. "If and when the rescuers come, boss, there will be people backing them up. I will take care of those as they come in. You go find Leo."

"I knew it!" Cody said. "You just can't go five minutes without having to issue orders to people!"

"Keep your voice down!" Bob hissed. "I thought I heard someone."

They waited a moment and voices reached them.

The sun peeped through the foliage and birds sounded, letting their neighbors know about claimed territory and the need for mates. Monkeys joined them and lemurs howled. Bob whispered, "I hate mornings out here!"

"We've got to move to where we can watch the road. Their noise can cover our noise."

"And the natives cannot tell the difference?" Bob asked.

214 | HALLEN TAYLOR

Cody turned and frowned. "Crawl quietly, Bob! There's no problem here unless you want to wake the world!"

Once they reached the road, they saw no people. Cody stood up and saw several heads north of them near the abandoned vehicles. They began to shout. One man turned and ran back south to report their findings. Cody waited and knocked him into Bob, who knocked him unconscious by striking the side of his neck.

Bob asked, "Now what, boss?"

Cody grinned. "We wait for the next one."

"Yeah," Bob agreed. "One at a time at this rate will only take about 500 years."

Their unconscious man stirred. Cody jumped the space between them and hit him again in the same area Bob had hit him. Cody said, "If Leo had hit him, I wouldn't have had to do that."

Bob sat down by the man lying flat across tall grass. "I think that I'm resigning this job, Cody. I don't want to work anymore. However, our work has been incredibly easy!"

Cody sat down and nodded his head without looking anywhere but his boots. "Okay, Bob, I'm sorry that I called you and Leo in on this business. I'm sorry I had no coffee for you at breakfast. Is there anything else I can say to keep you from resigning this morning or before our work is finished here?"

Bob thought carefully before responding. "Since you're still on probation, I think you might figure our next move or count on being dismissed at our debriefing in Bogota--if we manage to live through this mess that you got us into."

"Okay, Bob. Here's my take. I don't like it but I see no other choice. I hope you come up with something better."

"I'll let you know. Proceed."

Cody said, "This doesn't set well with me at all, but we cannot allow those guys to go back into their headquarters. We need at least one vehicle. So we're going to have to shoot them."

Bob nodded negatively. "That's not going to happen, Cody. Those people, armed or not, aren't professional soldiers. I think that it's best that we just walk away from this instead of killing innocents. We do, however, have to rescue Leo before they torture him."

Cody looked at the unconscious figure. "Let's tie him. I don't want to shoot him, either."

"How?" Bob asked.

Cody removed the man's shirt and moved him into a sitting position. He lifted the man's knees. He tied one sleeve to the man's wrist and brought it to meet the other hand under the knees. He wrapped the ankles tight with the body of the shirt and tied the other sleeve tightly around the other wrist. He jerked the ends of the sleeves extra tight.

Bob asked, "You think he can't escape from that old woman's way of tying him?"

"Can you do it better?"

Bob said, "No. But I admit he will spend a lot of time getting out of that mess."

Cody checked the barrel of his AK-47 for dirt and reloaded. Bob did the same in silence.

They walked toward the vehicles through the grass. The men all loaded into the back of the trucks.

Cody said, "I'll take the drivers. You take care of the men in the bed of the truck."

"Okay! But this time, Cody, actually fire your rifle!"

Cody shot the driver of the nearest pickup and then the passenger before jumping to one side to shoot the driver of another vehicle. Bob's weapon sounded almost like an automatic with is finger pulling the trigger one round at a time. Men wounded and dead fell over the sides.

Cody ran through the grass to shoot the one escaping. He shot once and that man fell. The two others dropped to their bellies. Cody shot them, also. He ran back in the direction of Bob, who had already run for the trucks.

They found some wounded among the dead and pulled them clear of the trucks. The wounded watched as they stretched the dead out after clearing them of the vehicles.

Cody stopped a lone man who had a shoulder wound and appearing to be in pain. He ripped a sleeve off his shirt and tied it tightly around the wound. He then spoke to him in Spanish:

"We are going to the headquarters and finish this battle. We do not want to fight you again. We will not shoot your women and children. We will shoot anyone, however, who chooses to pick up a weapon against us. These are our words and we speak the truth."

The wounded man nodded his understanding. "I will tell the others if they wake."

Bob said, "I don't have enough bullets to go back there!"

They quickly robbed each weapon they found of ammo. They filled two magazines each. Cody drove one of the trucks. He said before they got to the gate, "Let's bail before we reach the gate. We'll go in on foot after they come to inspect this loose vehicle. Let's give them a war they won't easily forget."

Bob said, "If we get out of this, I'm suing you for reckless endangerment."

"And I'll sue you for holding me back and getting in the way! Jump!

CHAPTER 26

They landed and ran in the brush on each side of the gate. The pickup slowed and idled into the corner of the nearest building. A few men ran to it. Others looked around cautiously. One man began to bark orders.

Four men with rifles ran to the gate side by side. Shortly before arriving, Cody and Bob shot two rounds each and all four men dropped almost simultaneously.

One man standing near the truck yelled for men to take cover. Most of them ran and were cut down. The last man to fall happened to be the man giving orders. He stood by the pickup and waited to yell at someone.

Women screaming and yelling filled the space around the men. They cried and wailed. When they quieted somewhat, Cody yelled to them.

"This ranch is surrounded! If you wish to leave this place, go! If you stay, you will be killed!"

A voice from inside the big house called to them. "You are only two men! We have one of the three of you. If you will surrender yourselves now, he will not be harmed. You will live to stand trial for murder. It will be a fair trial. The General of the Army has agreed to this. The president also agrees to this. You have ten minutes. The army will come. Your friend will be shot. You will be shot as the soldiers find you!"

THE CARTELS ERROR: BOOK FOUR OF THE CODY HUNTER SERIES | 219

Bob laughed in a whisper. He whispered as loud as possible. They have not notified anyone! He's bluffing! He also speaks without an accent. Do you know him?"

Cody spoke lowly. "No. But a bunch of these guys are lawyers that received their education in the United States. They learned English. Some remained in the U.S.A. Some come back to here to work for the cartels in Colombia!"

"They do have Leo, though."

Leo stood on top of the nearest building and attempted to get their attention. He waved frantically. He hope the bad guys didn't see him before Cody and Bob.

Cody called back to the spokesman. "Call the general of the army again. Tell him we will kill any soldier that comes after us! After we kill his army, we will use their weapons against you! We will level your house and we will burn your trees that yield your cocaine. The ten minutes you gave us are what we are giving you!"

They listened to the dead silence for ten minutes. The spokesman called to them. "Listen to me! We have called the general. He will not assemble his soldiers until tomorrow! You can remain outside and wait until tonight when we will send the dogs after you. Men with rifles will accompany them. Do you have questions for me? Will we harm you? No. You will be given the opportunity to stand trial. Of course, you will be found guilty of murder and be hanged later. What is your choice?"

"I choose to shoot your dogs and the men who accompany them. I also choose to fight the general's army! I choose to burn your houses! If you wish to escape, please try! This is my choice! Come out with your hands up!"

"There is an airplane arriving here in another forty-five minutes. Please do not fire on this aircraft. It will bring you no harm."

Cody walked back into the brush and crossed the road to Bob. "I hate to lose you, partner, but we've got to cover that airstrip. You want to flip for it?"

Bob shrugged. "I'll go. I might want to turn myself in and stand a fair trial because I ain't sleeping in no tree tonight!"

"The bugs and ants will kill you, Bob. Find a tree to sleep or else find a motel in town!"

"What are we going to do for food, Cody? We can't stay out here forever!"

"I'm sneaking into that compound tonight. I'll find Leo and arm him. One of us will find you and feed you. After you eat, we'll send for a nutritionist and see if we did well or not."

"Food and water, Cody, one has to have it to survive."

Cody shrugged. "I'm good and I haven't eaten since I was a small child! We will have a shower this morning or this afternoon. There will be water for drinking in that rain. I thought you ridge runners could be tough when the chips were down."

"Well, I ain't going to go without food!" Bob said.

"It really wouldn't hurt you, Bob, to go a few days without food. Okay! All right! Take off. Good luck on finding a burger house between here and the strip!"

Bob left at a trot. Cody felt sleepy.

The lawyer for the Montiago brothers stood in the doorway of Sasha's room, the man who could whip all of Russia and the entire European continent with his bare fists lay in bed as if both legs were missing. A bandage showing blood leakage from a smashed nose covered most of his face. The man showed obvious pain. The medic already reported the man refusing pain killers.

The lawyer stepped to the side of the dangerous Russian's bedside and saw him wide awake. Their eyes met with no greeting or satisfaction upon seeing one another. The lawyer waited a moment before sneering.

"Look at you!" he said in Spanish in order for the man to understand, who knew very little English. You are the man who rips limbs off other men! What good are you now? You received a punch in your face! Oh—my! Who are you going to beat? Give me one reason why I brought you here? You are a phony! You took our traveling money! I have wasted money on you! I tell you now, Russian. You are going to get up and leave these premises! You will receive no more money. You have embarrassed us! Rise and walk! I want you out of here!"

The broad-shouldered Russian sat up suddenly and groaned from the exertion. He stood wobbly until he regained at least a part of his composure. The lawyer took a step backward.

"I am Alexander (Sasha) Potnik Koschev! You will not talk to me in this bad manner! I am a champion fighter! This American faked an injury and punched me unexpectedly! He broke my nose in two places! I will kill him for this! Anyway, you stinking wretch of a man, I will kill you if you tell me one word from your mouth again! I am not leaving! I will earn my pay and I will collect the agreed amount of money from you! Are we clear on this or do I have to put you in this bed with broken bones?"

The lawyer pulled a .45 automatic sidearm from underneath his jacket. "If you move toward me, you will die!"

Sasha turned away and laughed scornfully. "Are you strong enough to pull the trigger? Ha! You are..."

The lawyer shot him once and watched his large body be violently hurled away from the impact of a heavy .45 caliber bullet. He shot him in the chest three more times and once in the head when he fell to the floor.

He turned to his subordinates who stood frozen and white faced. "Clean up this mess and burn this stupid man's body! Bury his bones deep in the field. Do not waste good bandages on such stupid men again!"

Leo heard the shots and walked back to the open window. Instead of escaping to the roof again, he decided to find an armed worker and take his weapon. He passed one open door and came to a closed one on the same side of the hallway. He opened it and found five teen-aged girls, who turned to him with surprised expressions. "Whoa--another group of you girls?"

The armed guard sitting among them quickly lifted his weapon to his shoulders.

Leo had already closed the distance between them by the time the wooden stock reached the man's shoulder. He kicked

THE CARTELS ERROR: BOOK FOUR OF THE CODY HUNTER SERIES | 223

the rifle away with his right foot and kicked the man in his face with the other foot. One girl had to scoot out of his way or be fallen upon.

Leo leaned back sleepily. "I am very tired! Oh--any of you girls speak English?"

The girl who had to move out of his way replied, "We all speak English, you big dummy! We are all United States citizens just like you! We were kidnapped and brought here against our will and we want to go home!"

Leo took a step back from her, looking confused. "Okay— Okay! Just cool it, kiddo! I didn't have a thing to do with your being here! But since we might be on the same side, I'll help you escape after we level this place. Does that meet with your satisfaction?"

She nodded her okay and looked at the man Leo had disarmed. He moaned and moved. Leo bent over slightly and swung the butt of the rifle against his face. It made a noise and the girls all let out a short scream.

Leo checked the clip for rounds and found one in the barrel. He shoved it back in place and kept it off safety. They watched him, eager for guidance. He stood still while he searched his brain for something positive to tell them.

"Okay, ladies! I'll need for you to stay here. I'm going to scout around and see what we're up against then I'll come back for you. There's another group of five just like you here somewhere from another ranch."

"The men!" one girl said. "They will come for us all day. I had rather die than to be touched by one of them again! I want to leave here, now!"

Leo backed up again and planned to argue but stepped into the hallway against his and the girl's wishes. He saw a group of men who looked straight at him. They all surrounded the lawyer. Without thinking, Leo fired into the group and raced in the opposite direction of the hallway. He left hearing all the girls screaming. He didn't get around the first corner when he met several more men. He fired five rounds into them before the slide remained open.

He didn't slow. While running two steps on the wall even with the men's heads, he snatched another rifle. He hit the door behind them and had no idea what direction he would take. A large truck in front of the doorway blocked his vision. He ran two steps and dived under it. He slid on the hard surface underneath and began firing. Bullets peppered the ground at his heels. He spun and fired at the group's legs. Some of them dropped. He scrambled underneath the truck and stopped between the dual wheels but underneath the low differential.

This is when he noticed the opened slide on his rifle. He saw a pair of feet close to the truck and he grabbed the ankles and pulled. He heard the man yell. He jerked the surprised man to him and secured the rifle before he lifted the back of the man's head upward and dropped him after his face collided with the iron works of the bed. He slid back and kicked the man's head again.

Guards dropped to their bellies searching for him. Thankfully, he noted it darker underneath than the bright sunshine outside. He fired into their faces on both sides of the truck and quickly looked behind. He shot one man as he dropped to the ground.

He scooted to the outside and snatched another rifle off a dead man. He noted this one had been issued a thirty-round magazine instead of ten. He kept firing fast, sometimes blind. He liked his new weapon. They backed off. It would only be seconds before someone rolled a grenade underneath the truck.

He heard the loud lawyer raise his voice above the crowd. "Stupid American!" he began. "Do you think you can hide under that truck all day?"

Leo remained quiet. He bent low and found feet and legs at a distance all the way around except the front. If they tossed a grenade one at a time, he might have time to retrieve it and toss it back. Otherwise, he thought he might be on the losing end of the game again.

The angry voice reached him again. "We are giving you one last chance to surrender yourself! My men have grenades!"

Leo spoke. "Wait, *jefe*! I wish to surrender myself!"

"Very well!" the loud voice sounded. "Show your hands without the weapons!"

"Wait!" Leo argued. "I wish to have a fair trial right now."

The lawyer laughed. "Of course you will have a fair trial. Then you will be hanged lawfully with much respect!"

CHAPTER 27

Shooting from outside the truck suddenly erupted. Leo dropped his head as low as possible to see who shot at him after he promised to surrender. He saw many bodies fall. Surprised, he moved his unconscious guard and peered from underneath. The shooting came from one man behind the bed of a pickup.

"It's either Cody or Bob," Leo thought, and fired into the legs of people standing, running for the doors to the big house, and falling. Cody kept firing while Leo emptied the rounds remaining in his clip. During the heaviest firing, he ran for the pickup where Cody fired and sailed over the entire bed and slid behind him as if saved by sliding home from third base.

Cody stopped and turned. He made a grab for Leo's collar to jerk him to his feet. They ran at top speed through the gate and into the trees without anyone firing at them.

Leo panted hard. He threw both hands against a large tree trunk and gasped. "Cody," he began, pausing between breaths, where's Bob and where have you been? Did you know that I've been holding these guys off me all night from underneath that truck?"

"Leo," Cody said, keeping his breath under control. "I've asked you a hundred times to not ever waste bullets. Now before you start denying it, Bob is at the airfield. He is hungry. I wish you had a sandwich or something for him."

"For him?" Leo asked unbelievably. "What about me? I'm already weak from starvation! You go in there and fix him a sandwich! Go ahead. Grab one for me and a flour tortilla for yourself!"

Cody checked his weapon. "I can't do it. I'm afraid I'd put mustard on yours instead of mayo. I don't even know if you prefer turkey over ham or not."

Leo said, "Cody, for the sake of sanity, leave the humor to me!"

Cody grinned and agreed. "You got it, old buddy! What's that?"

"What's what?" Leo asked, still panting hard.

"Shhh!" Cody shushed harshly. "Listen!"

They both did and the sound came louder and frightening! "Helicopters!" Leo said excitedly.

They watched as three loaded Huey 500's flew over the main house and landed in the big yard. Cody climbed a tree and watched with his glasses. "They're army birds but they ain't troops!"

"What, then?" Leo asked. "Why is the army here? Are they here to help us?"

Cody watched as well-armed civilians unloaded and began hugging the guards remaining at the Montiago ranch. "No. Looks like it's going to be right the opposite, Leo."

Leo walked a few paces toward the house and looked back. "Been nice knowing you, Cody!"

Cody felt puzzled, "Wha—what?"

Leo cackled with laughter. "I was going to join the enemy, but seeing the look on your face, I changed my mind! My, but you looked pitiful! Now that's funny!"

Leo laughed more and said, "Don't ever let me tell you that you aren't funny, Cody!"

Cody dropped to the ground and said, "Leo, we have a major problem!"

Leo sat down at the base of a tree still sniggering. "What problem? Wrapping things up here at this ranch ain't happening. Now we have how many more people to fight, sixty? Seventy?"

Cody replied, "Oh—about twenty-five, considering they carried eight men in each chopper. They not only have rifles, they have big guns, rocket launchers and real bazookas. We need to get back to town and resupply our ammo. I'm out. I'm sure you wasted all your rounds, too."

Leo said, "No doubt about it. These guys' bosses don't believe in giving them a lot of rounds. It's no wonder they can't shoot straight. But this ain't our big problem, Cody."

"So tell me the problem, boy."

"The girls, Cody. You may not know about them, but I do. I just left them a half-hour ago."

"What about them, Leo? You're talking like they're our problem."

"They are our problem, Cody. All of them were kidnapped from their schools, or nearby on their way home. High school girls! Right out of L.A.'s finest schools!"

Cody looked at him questionably. "Finest schools? In L.A? Are you talking L.A., California?"

"Cut it out, Cody! I don't want to hear your right wing, Karate, Kung Fu blabbering. These are young girls who have been kidnapped from their schools and from their parents. We are not leaving them here!"

Cody felt embarrassed. Leo, the joker, had the same dry tone in humor as he did in seriousness. "Of course we cannot leave them, Leo. How many are there, a hundred?"

"Ten."

Cody chuckled, "That's all? We'll haul them out of here with seats left over."

"Not in a helicopter, you won't. They just bounced out of here."

Cody found another way to redeem himself. "Bob is watching over the airplane that arrived a little while ago. We'll borrow that one. If it isn't large enough, we'll get to town and steal a larger one."

"I don't care what you do, Cody. I'll take one sedans here and load up five. Dan can take another sedan and haul the other five."

Cody liked the idea but it sounded weak. "Do you know how many check points there are between here and Mexico where each one of you will have to explain what you're doing with young girls. No one will have the money to get you through the checkpoints. When you get to Mexico, if you can make it that far, not even the U. S. Government has the money to buy you through each checkpoint. You will either die from bullets or in jail. I will fly the girls home."

"Not with me, you ain't."

Cody felt hurt again. "Fine! You can walk home."

"Better than dying in a plane crash."

Cody said, "I am not going crash, Leo."

Leo shook his head frantically. "You will! You will! You will crash the airplane and you know you will! I can tell when you're lying, Cody, and you're lying right now!"

Cody muttered, "Jeeze, Leo. All of those crashes in Iraq were on purpose with my hands and feet on the controls. No one was ever injured."

"I was there, Cody. In each crash you were rolled up in a ball on the floor with your arms clamped tight around your head each time you crashed. Bob saw you and we dragged you out of the aircraft with you screaming, "Fasten your seat belts!" We always had a hard time slapping you out of the hysterics."

"More Leo humor," Cody thought, and began to talk sober to Leo. "Okay, Leo. But we have to keep this a little secret among ourselves. Okay? The girls need not know."

"Of course not, Cody, I don't share our team secrets."

Cody sat down and tossed a handful of dirt against the ground. "What, Leo? What can we do? We don't have weapons or anything to fight with. Tonight, they'll be searching the trees here with night vision goggles. Without guns, Leo, we'll be easy targets for them."

"Oh—yeah! Hang in there, Cody! I've always loved your 'Never say quit' attitude."

"You got any ideas, Leo?"

"No. I cannot think with your negative thinking spilling all over everything around here!"

"Well, first of all, we cannot fight without weapons. That means we have to borrow them from the enemy. Safety isn't in numbers in our situation, Leo. We're going to have to split up."

"Thank goodness for that!" Leo said. "I just barely can take care of myself!"

"Okay, Bob's at the airstrip complaining about the lack of food and water. We'll have water to drink this afternoon. But, anyway, he's slightly east of us and a quarter mile south, if not more. If you take the east side, just remember he's there. I'll take the right or west section."

Leo thought about it and agreed. "I'm going to walk north and at least a half-mile east. I'll close in on the eastern side of them once they start hunting us."

"Likewise," Cody said. "Don't get cocky, Leo. Let everything happen naturally."

"Oh—sure! Coming from Mr. Showmanship, himself! I'm apt to get cocky? Okay, here's the deal, Cody. You make sure that you don't walk several miles west and remove yourself out of all the action!"

Cody rolled his eyes upward. "We both know that I'll have to work both my side and yours."

Leo chuckled. "When do we meet back here? I mean this exact location."

"We'll meet after the show's over, but not here. I don't even know where we're at."

Leo thought a moment and said, "Cody? I'm sorry, son, but we have another problem, a real change of plans."

"Oh yeah? What's that?"

"We can't leave those teenagers here one more night. These new guys are apt to kill them or maim them for life."

Cody sighed deeply and agreed. "How do we work it, Leo?"

"Well, you know me, partner, I'm the one who always says the best laid plans are a waste of time and effort. We'll play it by ear."

Cody nodded. "That's what I figured. It will be easier if we let the troops walk passed us and go in after dark."

"Do you think that they'll come for us today? This very afternoon?"

Cody nodded, "Why not? It's the new guys' chance to shine. They will come shortly after the sun goes down or after it's very dark."

Leo said, "Night vision glasses! Daylight for them, darkness for us."

"All right, listen up, Leo. Those latest glasses have two ranges, close ups and distance. In these trees, they're apt to use either one or be changing them all the time. They aren't infa—red, they're just light gatherers. Get on the outside of the people, Leo. "

"I got you! But we need to get to the big house fast if we're going to help the girls."

"Pay attention, Leo! Let's say there are thirty new troops. Half will go east of the road, the other half will take the west side. They will walk fifty feet apart or closer, much closer due to the trees. My question for you is how far do I walk west to be on the west side of them?"

Leo said, "Duhh! I can't figure that without paper. We will have to use a knife on them or else strangle them without them thrashing about. I don't even have a knife."

"Me, neither! We'll have to use our fists."

Leo chuckled. "You couldn't knock a chicken unconscious, Cody."

Cody grinned at him. "Okay, how do we arm ourselves?"

"We don't. We're going to go the camp unarmed and arm ourselves there. These new guys will be gone for hours, walking northward or in a close proximity of the ranch headquarters. Right now, let's both get west of what we think is coming. About a quart-mile should do it."

"That's the dumbest idea you've ever had, Leo."

Leo asked, "Do you have anything better?"

"No."

Late that afternoon, clouds formed and a shower peppered them with rain for five minutes. They made funnels from large leaves and drank their fill. Both men had been thirsty. They used surface mud to cover their light hair and face.

"You're a remarkable improvement, Cody!"

"Zip it, Leo. I'm worried."

"Worrying doesn't help. Thinking helps. Try it, Cody."

"Worrying is thinking, Leo! Now hush yourself while I muddle through this."

Leo hummed to himself and drummed his knee.

Cody picked a large leaf, half dead, and backhanded Leo across the chest with it. Leo jumped and almost yelled.

Once he settled, Leo said, "You scared me! You can think half your brain away and you still can't come up with anything better than what I planned. Hey! There's a hundred little bugs crawling all over my chest! Cody—you dummy!"

CHAPTER 28

Shortly before the shower that afternoon, Bob worked his way around the end of the dirt runway where the airplane stood. A twin-engine turbo prop stood magnificently as if in flight. One man guarded it. He sat in the shade it provided and moved when its shadow moved.

Bob melted into the thick vegetation and spent more than two hours carefully crawling through the leaves covering most of the ground and branches. Creepy things of the forest floor caused his skin to crawl and itch. During the shower, the guard rose up and fashioned himself a funnel from a large leaf and drank. Bob used this time to get closer and jumped to rush the man.

The guard turned in time to partially see and feel the impact of a swift and powerful fist to the side of his neck and lower chin. He dropped his rifle but it never touched the earth. Bob caught it and checked the clip for rounds. He counted five and searched the man for anything usable.

He found a pair of old and rusty handcuffs for the man. "Great!" he thought and dragged him to the door of the aircraft. He found an empty place at the front of the pilot's seat. He cuffed him there. The man appeared to be sleeping soundly.

He searched his pockets for a key and found it. After exploring the aircraft's luggage and side pockets, he found a candy bar from the United States and ate it.

He found lots of American change and a few bills of Colombian money. He wanted food not money! When the guard began to stir, he stepped from the airplane and left the door open in order to provide him air.

With mud plastered over both their bodies, Cody and Leo began their long hike across the wide parking lot. The open parking seemed safe, even if several men lounged in front of the main building.

As the guards noticed the pair walking toward them, covered with mud, they straightened and readied their rifles.

Cody said, "You better let me do the talking. They're going to notice that we aren't from their bunch if you talk English with a Boston accent."

Leo shrugged. "Could be they're thinking we are of the new batch."

"Whatever. Don't wave, just walk directly toward them."

Leo said, "I'm beginning to think this is not a very good idea."

Cody grinned. "I tried to tell you that but you insisted."

One guard called to them in Spanish. "What happened?"

Cody opened his arms and half turned while he kept walking. "They ambushed us!"

Three more guards leveled their rifles at them. "When?"

"While the water fell from the sky! Only a kilometer to the north! There was an army of them!"

"An army!" The spokesman looked around at the others. They grinned broadly, showing their white teeth. "I think you are mistaken, my friend! We are the army. We are in pursuit of three men who fight like they are an army."

Cody threw his arms into the air. "Three men! Impossible! Three men cannot cover four sides!"

"Four sides?" The spokesman laughed loudly. "Oh—I think I understand. One of your men from Los Palomas became confused. It was he who made the fourth man."

All the guards laughed and lowered their weapons.

Cody stopped and stamped one foot. He threw up one arm and lowered it to his waist. He leaned over to the spokesman and motioned for him to come forward. "You think this is a joke? Come to me and tell me that we are a joke! Come on!"

"What?" the spokesman said. "You are insulted? The errors are yours!"

Cody and Leo both lowered their heads and motioned them forward. Leo asked Cody, "Do you really think you can take this guy with all the others supporting him, Cody?"

Cody ignored him and challenged all of them. He counted nine. "Come! All of you! You think you can laugh at us? Come, I will teach you manners!"

Three of the nine dropped their rifles and began walking passed the spokesman, who said, "Are you crazy?"

Cody whispered, "Leo, follow my lead. We'll get all of them out here. Maybe more will drop their weapons to make the fight fair."

Leo responded in a harsh whisper. "You dumb *gringo!* I am not on your side!"

Cody taunted the guards. He ran toward them and stopped. When he saw all of them coming, he turned and ran back a few steps. Leo stayed right with him. All of the guards dropped their weapons and ran toward Cody and Leo the moment they started running.

The guards swarmed them in seconds. Cody went down first. He ignored the blows to his sides and head while he pushed a part of them back. The spokesman still had his weapon. Cody kicked and punched as he made his way for the spokesman who noted the color of Cody's hair when someone pulled mud from it. He pushed one man into the spokesman and sent himself forward with all the speed he could muster. The spokesman went down. Cody got his right hand on the rifle and blindly pushed himself forward again, desperately throwing his left fist at anyone showing his face.

Once he cleared the crowd, he found the spokesman still clinging to his rifle. He yelled as loud as possible. "It is them, the *gringos!* Run for your rifles and kill them! Hurry!"

Cody kicked the man's head and the rifle came free. He noted two men running the few yards to their weapons. Cody shot both of them from his hip.

Leo thrashed and angrily knocked men out of his way as he would with light bags of potatoes. One of his ears bled profusely from where it was almost torn from his head. It not only pained him, it angered him to where he lost all his humor. He had found a rifle and used the butt to lay all the men down that he encountered. Only a few men stood. They stopped at the sound of gunfire and lifted their hands to the air. Leo turned to Cody with the most dangerous face he ever carried.

Cody noted only two men standing. They others lay still on the ground. He used their language. "Get on your knees put your hands over your heads!"

"Are you going to kill us, *gringo*?" one of the men asked.

Cody answered him in Spanish. "Why not?"

They turned to face him on their knees. "Because we have families!"

Cody nodded and held the rifle steadily. "Very well," he replied. "We will not kill you."

"This is true?" both men replied. "The war is over between us. True?"

Cody grinned. "It is much better that way, my friends. Go! Hide yourselves in the forest until the fighting is over. Then come back for your families. Find work at another place. If we see you again, you will die."

Both men scrambled to their feet and ran for the forest. Leo came to him and frowned. "I hope we didn't make a mistake, Cody."

"As I do so hope mightily, Leo. Let's get inside before you lose half your hearing!"

They made their way down a hall familiar to Leo, who held a finger to his lips. An unnecessary gesture Cody thought, and looked quickly in front and behind them, ready to fire at the first movement. After turning to the right at the first intersection of hallways, Leo swiftly bounced across the hallway and opened the door to the room of young girls. They uttered half screams but two of them quickly ran to Leo and set him down on a bed.

"I assume these are the young girls," Cody said. "I'll have to watch from the outside. Maybe they can attach your ear back to your head."

Leo frowned and flinched when one touched his ear. One found a towel and began to try to stop the bleeding. Another said it would stop bleeding once they applied a tight bandage.

Leo motioned for Cody to sit. Just give me a second here, Cody. You're always leaving me behind. Relax!"

Cody sat on the corner of a bed where he could watch the two doors leading into the room from two hallways. "How often do they come in here?" he asked.

The youngest looking and the tiniest said, "They don't come so often in the daytime. At night they are in and out of here, taking us with them."

Cody shook his head sadly. "They have no dignity, little sister. They are not men."

"We know but what can we do?"

Cody remained silent.

The same girl asked him, "Do you know the rich *gringo* that comes here often?"

"No. Who is this rich *gringo?*"

"We don't know his name. He comes here often."

"How often and from where does he come?"

"He will not tell us. We just know that he wants all of us in one night. We go one at a time."

Cody nodded. "About what time does he come for you?"

"Right after dinner. Aside from the lawyer who runs this place for the rich Montiago brothers, he has second choice over us after the lawyer has his choice."

Leo smiled for the first time. One of the girls ripped a clean bedsheet and wrapped his head tightly. She had no disinfectant.

"Cody, what do you say that we join these guys for dinner and make a few choices on how to kill them?"

Cody liked the idea but turned it down. "We'll wait for them here. After all have come for their choices, we will develop a plan and play it by ear.

"Do what you can to lift these girls' spirits." Cody suggested. "Make them believe you are comedian or something."

The girl who wrapped Leo's head looked up. "These brutal men hit us when we attempt to avoid them. We are their slaves."

Cody's heart went out to them. He lowered his head and found it unbelievable on how cowardly some men can be.

CHAPTER 29

Bob searched the entire airplane again. He found many papers, all carried Washington D.C.'s addresses. A few Colombian papers had fresh dates on them. His prisoner awoke cautiously, watching him intently. Bob thought of two different things his prisoner wanted, to talk or to die.

Bob glanced at him and grunted, "What?"

"Do you know Spanish?" the man asked in his native tongue from his uncomfortable position on the floor.

Bob knew enough to figure the question. "No. You speak English or silence yourself."

From the papers Bob read, this airplane belonged to no one. Business papers scattered about told him nothing except that a few bogus companies claiming D.C. addresses. It appeared that the pilot smuggled cocaine from Bogota to unknown points in the U.S.A. However, he found no traces of cocaine or marijuana anywhere in the aircraft. Perhaps the pilot only set up deals.

"*Senor!*" The man wanted Bob's attention again.

"English!" Bob demanded.

"Yes! Yes!" the man muttered. "*Tengo unas pocas palabras en Igles!*"

Bob understood but had little to no patience with the man. "Use them!" he ordered.

"You—you kill me?"

Bob looked at him rather puzzled. "If it's necessary. Now shut up!"

The man looked at him in horror and then his face relaxed. "Shut *ap! Silencio?*"

Relieved that the man could communicate a few words, he said again. "It is possible that I will kill you."

Disappointment covered the man's face again. Then he relaxed. "Maybee! *Verdad?* True?"

Bob nodded. He showed the man his fist and used the Spanish word he just learned, which meant the same in Italian. "Silence! *Silencio!*"

The man nodded his understanding. "*Gracias!* Thank you, *senor!*"

Bob saw no other choice. He opened his hand and slapped the man's face once. "Silence! *Graci!* Thank you!"

This time the red-faced prisoner held his tongue, although his respect for Bob diminished.

Bob sat in a chair in the sweltering heat inside the airplane more than three hours. He saw no other form of life in the jungle. The sun moved to the west but the heat grew more stifling.

"*Senor!*" the man said in a pained voice. "*Quiero tirar agua! Es nesessario por me a tirar agua!* I—I wan' pee pee!"

Bob understood the English part of the last sentence. He got up and found the rusting handcuff key. The handcuff on the chair came loose and the man almost got up with Bob partially on top of him. He held on to the empty handcuff while the prisoner hurried to the door, opened his fly and let go. Bob pitied the man for having no manners. He wished it would rain. He needed a drink of water.

No sooner had he thought it when a cloud formed over them and boomed with the sound echoing across their sky. A light shower soaked them. They still had time to build a funnel and drink. Their bellies were full by the time the rain stopped and the sky cleared itself of the temporary obstruction blotting part of its perfect blue.

Bob felt sleepy and needed to lie down. He moved the reluctant prisoner to the floor again and handcuffed him to a front seat. This time he searched the man's pockets for wire or anything he could use for a key. After this, he stretched out on the floor and closed his eyes. Sleep came fast.

Cody looked at the blood-stained bandage stretched across Leo's head and ear. We're going to have to abandon this project and get you to a doctor! This doesn't look good."

"Mind your own business you old woman!" Leo said sharply.

"I am! Whether you can fight or not has a direct bearing on my well-being!"

Leo chuckled. "You got that right! But I've always taken care of you, right?"

"Yes! When I wasn't taking care of you, you always watched over me. Right now, I'm watching over you!"

Leo scoffed. "I'm in big trouble."

The young teenagers looked at them with worried faces. One of them asked Leo. "Do you not like this man? I thought you were friends."

"Nothing to worry about, little sister." Cody said. "We are friends. I would allow him to marry my sister if I had one, for which I'm very grateful for not having."

Leo fought back a painful expression. "Cody, will you stop with the stupid humor? You really worry me sometime."

"Don't start arguments in front of the young ladies, Leo! They don't understand your crude humor."

"When my ear heals, I'm going to give you a lesson in crudeness."

Cody chuckled. "Does that mean you'll be milking this painful ear thing for years?"

Leo chuckled. "Stop acting brave in front of these young ladies, Cody."

They heard noise in the hallway. Cody slid under a bed. Leo slid under another. The lawyer entered the room without knocking. "Dress in clean clothes over your clean bodies, my lovelies! Dinner is thirty minutes from now."

Bob's nap proved restless and short. He shook his head to clear it and decided to do something. Cody and Leo could be dead or they might be captured and in big trouble. Doing something didn't mean it was the right thing. He simply refused to sit around and wait for the enemy or for his partners to come for him.

He removed the handcuff to the seat's leg and led his prisoner outside. He had to get rid of him, somehow, but how? If he cuffed him to a tree, a large animal might happen along. Darkness closed in fast. He walked to the tree line and climbed. His prisoner, although handicapped climbed well. At the highest large limb, he followed it to another large limb that the handcuff would fit around. No man could bend such a limb and once the prisoner was secured, he climbed down.

Bob heard the man make several pleading sentences. He turned and said, "*Dos hores!*

The prisoner, at least 12 feet off the ground, nodded. "*Dos hores! Por seguro! Muchas gracias, senor!*"

Bob thought he would have to climb the tree again to save the man from wildlife possibilities, so he climbed. While doing so, he hoped that no jaguar or large snake would climb the tree. He wasn't familiar with the country, so he removed the handcuff from the tree and secured him to the pilot's seat again. This time he closed the door. Without the sun, the inside would be tolerable. With the door closed, the man would be safe from the wildlife, he hoped.

After the girls left for dinner, Cody asked Leo if they should make a stand in the girls' room or in the room of the lawyer of the Montiagos.

Leo thought a bit and said they come after the girls one at a time all night long.

Cody had already decided that. "Okay, Leo, fine, we're going to put the lights out for those who come for the girls. We still have to fight the remaining men."

"That we will, *compadre*! They'll come after us in a horde. We can manage them better my way."

"Suits me, Leo. I don't know but I'll bet, somehow, this won't go as planned. How much ammo do you have?"

I have twenty-five rounds total. They're in a thirty-round clip. You?"

"I have twenty or twenty-five. Now listen to me, Leo, this is important! I don't want to see you firing automatic cover rounds! That's a waste of ammo. I want each round you fire to bring down one or more men. No wasted ammo."

"Check! No wasted ammo, boss!"

Cody looked at him in the shadows of lights. "There are forty to sixty men out there that will literally fill us with bullets. We can't afford one wasted round."

Although hidden from Cody, Leo nodded in agreement.

The girls returned from dinner all in one group. Leo sat behind two girls on one bed. One of them said, "They will come for us any moment now." She began to weep.

Two others joined her. Leo patted her shoulders. "We will make our stand here, Cody!"

Cody stood by the door and waited. The girls all made sobbing sounds. Their hell would begin any moment. Cody heard heavy footsteps coming for the door.

The door swung open and Cody snatched him by the collar and jerked him inside. The man yelled before losing consciousness. Cody said to him, and grinned, "Not tonight, sweetie."

The man dropped to the floor. Two more men rushed inside, both asking what was happening. Both men dropped at the same time. No other people sounded in the hall. Cody didn't know if they had been spotted or not. Actually, he didn't care. He didn't mind fighting this type of men.

The girls cheered modestly, mostly in silence. They pointed to the man with light hair. "There is the *gringo!* Do you know him?"

"I'm afraid not, little sister," Cody said. "I don't think that I'd admit it if I did."

"This man here is the lawyer. He runs this place. He is very cruel!"

Leo stepped up and kicked the unconscious lawyer's head. "He's going to be a well behaved gentleman for the next few days." He kicked the same man in the face again. "Am I not right, sir?"

They pulled the men under the two beds. In a few more minutes, two more slowly opened the door. "Anyone here?" they asked in their native language. As they stepped inside grinning broadly, they, too, dropped the same as the others. One of the men dropped on his back, still conscious. Two girls jumped on him and began kicking him. They soon learned that they brought no harm to the man, one of them stamped hard on his genitals. The man yelled and sat straight up. Leo knocked him back down from the front and his head bounced off the floor. Leo kicked his head to make sure the man slept.

"Go home to your wives!" Leo said, feeling exasperated.

Leo said to the girls as they looked up at him. "When they wake up, hit their heads hard with this." He picked up a chair and ripped its legs off. He gave them each a leg. The fifth one, the smallest, he gave a lamp. "Hit them hard, ladies. Pretend their heads are made of rock and try to break it."

CHAPTER 30

Cody led the way through the hall. Leo walked with his left elbow against his back while he covered who might show behind them. Cody felt a deep sensation in his stomach, not sour but almost sickening. A lot of men would be dying moments from that time and he feared he and Leo would be among them.

Nothing happened. Leo nudged his back for attention. "If you see a man, shoot him."

Cody had no desire for any of Leo's humor, but laughter seemed the best ointment at the time. "Do you mean I need to shoot first?"

"Yes!" he answered in a harsh but low whisper. "You are not obligated to follow U.S. Civil Service Codes under these dangerous conditions."

"You're sure about that?"

"Cody, have you been seeing men and letting them go?"

"Dozens," he responded seriously, "but they were only armed guards."

Leo failed to appreciate Cody's humor. Laughter wasn't lifting the tension. He stopped at a closed doorway and listened. No sounds. They pressed on for a few seconds then froze from the sound of heavy gunfire."

They both looked at one another. Leo said innocently, "That cannot be me doing that shooting outside! I'm right here! Right, Cody?"

They bounded forward. Leo didn't look back. Cody, you don't need to lead me so fast!"

They rounded a corner and had time to see the backs of several men firing before them. Cody kicked the door wide open under the bright light above. He fired to his left with his rifle on full auto. Leo did the same from his right. In less than two seconds the last of the men fell, while they both froze. Leo turned to look behind him and began firing single rounds. By the time Cody turned while clicking from the full auto position, three men out of several fell. Cody joined Leo and felt the wind of two bullets as they passed.

The air's impact dazed him slightly but he fired as Leo fired and another ten men had fallen silently to the floor.

Cody stopped and ran back into their first melee and searched the bodies for another rifle. He found one with the slide open.

He lifted it and felt a heavy jolt against him. He fell against the wall and had dropped the rifle. By the time his senses returned, he saw Bob grinning above him and felt his strong grip lift him by his collar. Leo turned with the barrel of rifle passed Bob's stomach.

"Identify yourself!" Leo demanded, even though he could see Bob clearly.

All three men moved cautiously toward the unconscious men. All appeared either dead or seriously wounded. They

252 | HALLEN TAYLOR

collected clips from the rifles. For safety, they opened the chambers and collected the single rounds, also.

A call from around a corner reached them. "*Javier, que paso?*"

They froze as Cody responded to the call. "I'm not Javiar! He is very dead! Hurry!"

Three men slid around the corner and froze as bullets struck their chests. They wore side arms as well as carrying rifles.

Cody ejected the clips from two before Bob snatched the other to perform the same thing. They took the time to reload those clips. Cody, happy that he had not used the fresh thirty rounds he now carried in his large clip. Leo did the same. Bob simply filled his ten-round clip and stuffed his pant pockets with several rounds.

They stood up and Leo slapped Bob on the shoulder. "For once, I'm happy to see you, boss! I needed some help in keeping Cody under control and safe at the same time."

"He's no longer our problem, Leo. I'm not approving his probation extension again."

"That saddens me, deeply," Cody said dryly. "I have already resigned but I got caught up in this mess. Don't expect me to help you guys anymore."

"That's a relief!" Leo sighed. "But go ahead and keep that rifle and ammo in case Bob and I might want to borrow it later."

"Let's head back for the girls' room," Cody suggested. "That *gringo* pilot needs to answer a few questions before he flies us out of here."

"Bob looked at him questionably. "I thought you might do that for us."

Cody grinned. "I'm superstitious, Bob. I've crashed every South American aircraft I've ever piloted."

Leo said, "Cody, you have crashed every airplane you've ever flown."

"Have not!" Cody argued. "I never crashed one airplane in flight school."

Leo scoffed. "You can't prove that."

Bob chuckled and nudged both their shoulders. "We can argue after we've cleaned this place."

They walked to the girls' room and opened the door. Five men lay on the floor. All but the *gringo* slept as if unconscious.

The girls all suppressed screams and pleased emotions as they filed into the room.

The oldest said, "I never thought that I would ever be glad to see three old men in my life!"

Leo grinned and said, "The show isn't over just yet, little sister."

Cody kicked the foot of the *gringo* on the floor. If you have a name other than scumbag, mister, let's have it."

The man looked up, apparently not pleased with whom he had to talk. "Who're you? And if you kick my foot again, guns or not, you're going to get your teeth realigned."

Cody grinned. "Slow down, scumbag! We are not the police from back home, so you don't have to act so brave. Now, I won't ask again. Let's see some identification and tell us what you're doing, which includes why you're here raping and torturing these young teenagers."

The man sat up and regretfully responded. "If you aren't D.E.A. or Customs, I don't have to tell you anything!"

Cody used his fist to knock him flat on his back again. "Right!—but only up to a point. You don't talk again until I tell you. I'd advise you to answer truthfully. Never mind the lack of tact used here. This is not being recorded. Also be advised that if I have to take you out of this room, you will have your chance to realign my teeth."

Leo spoke up, "In case you didn't get the drift of what he just said to you, mister, you two will fight one on one. I doubt if you'd like that."

The American nodded with pleasure. "You're already missing one tooth. I'll square the other side up for you."

Cody thought about that and objected. "Please, if you don't mind. Dental bills are atrocious during these crazy times."

Cody searched him and found a wallet. He carried nothing else but a gold necklace and pocket knife. He went through the wallet and found several U. S. bills. He counted almost seven hundred dollars in fifties and twenties. He tossed it to the oldest girl.

"Divide this among you."

"Okay, scumbag. Your Arizona Driver's License says that you are Morris Gunther Walters. I don't see anything relating to a pilot's credentials. What's your business here?"

"I'm only a messenger. I don't do anything physical."

"Is that all you've got to say?"

"No. Who're you guys if you ain't feds?"

Cody lifted him and threw him back against the wall. "You are a conspirator. If you're lucky, I'll turn you over to the D.E.A. with everything they need to bring you up on charges. They cannot make you talk later but I can right now. You'll tell me everything about yourself, from the size of your grandma's dentures to your first arrest in the states. All of this will happen before we leave. I love you tough guys."

"Guys, we need to get back to matters at hand." Leo suggested.

Cody kicked the *gringo's* ribs once he lowered him to the floor. "I'm sorry for the kick, Mr. Walters. I don't want you to get physical with the little girls, again."

"You won't be able to use it in court." The man said.

Cody scoffed at him. "Who cares if you go to jail or not? You'll spend the rest of your life in a bed eating from a tube in your arm, anyway."

They stopped even with the door and waited. Cody looked back in the direction they came. "I don't like this, guys, but one of us is going to remain here with the girls to protect them."

Leo said, "I'll stay. They trust me because I'm not violent."

"We still don't know how many we are up against." Cody said. The guards in the forest will number about twenty or so. They'll be back tonight. At any rate, we have to erase the Montiago heads and set the business on fire. We need to count on being out of here before daylight in the morning."

Bob agreed. "The sooner the better!"

Cody and Bob sat silently at the open door for an hour. Suddenly, out of the brush came a gunshot. Both he and Bob saw the muzzle flash in the darkness. At the same time, they heard the large sound of the bullet hitting the light bulb above their heads.

They now had to depend upon the stars for light, as did the approaching guards. They waited several moments while expecting a rush.

The brush seemed to be getting closer to them, Cody thought, and studied it carefully. Sure enough, one large bush seemed to have left the line of brush behind it. He leaned over cautiously to Bob.

"They have night vision but they don't want to walk here in force. I am assuming they can't see us behind these walls by the door. Let's allow the first two or three to enter, then we take them out before the rush comes."

Bob nodded in the silence and darkness and pushed Cody back to a better position. They waited.

Finally, two figures, one at a time, rushed inside the door and squatted. Cody and Bob controlled themselves well. The last one whispered loudly. *"Esta bien!"*

Cody and Bob moved in unison. They hit each of the scouts in the face and slammed their heads against the concrete floor. They would use the rifles of these men first.

They rush came fast. They couldn't see until ten feet away and they barely had time to pull the triggers. Men fell in the door. Cody and Bob switched their weapons to full automatic and shot as many people in the dark as possible. Many men, perhaps half, escaped back into the brush for safety.

They found two night vision devices among those down. They took the rifles back inside and collected more ammunition and full clips. After fitting the night vision goggles over their heads, they walked back to the girls' room.

Leo, relieved to hear the report, agreed that the remainder of the guards would hold off attacking the house until daylight. In the meantime, Cody and Bob walked back to the kitchen in the dark with their goggles. They needed matches and fuel.

The Montiago brothers met them in a hallway. They wanted to surrender themselves to the invaders of their home. One asked in surprisingly good English, "Who are you?"

Bob answered, "We are the men you wanted dead. Now, you are going to lose your house, plantation, your life and your friends, but not necessarily in that order."

He responded calmly. "Permit me and my brothers and his son to walk out of here. We will not start our cocaine business again. We will live in peace with the people of our country. Would you please allow us this favor? We can pay you."

Bob looked at Cody. "What's your thinking? Do you care if they start another business or not?"

Cody said, "They have been beaten. If they give us reason to return, we will execute them."

Bob said, "You are right, although a little over confident. I'm resigning from this mess."

Cody said, "As I am." He patted both men down for weapons and found nothing. He sat them on the floor by a door and advised them to sit until daylight in the event another attack came.

The Montiagos wisely said nothing. They felt gratitude toward the Americans for allowing them to live, especially after hiring men to kill them.

Cody and Bob walked to the kitchen area.

CHAPTER 31

They both heard the shuffling on the opposite side of the closed door at the same time. Cody leaped far ahead and turned back to face Bob in mid-air with the rifle pointed at the closed door. Bob dropped to his stomach while pointing his rifle in the same direction as the door crashed open.

A professional guard for the highly successful Montiago Cartel could have used more caution and perhaps lived through his last dash for freedom. He roared like a lion as he plunged through the doorway, breaking most of the door that opened in front of him. He held two .44 magnums and fired wildly, hoping to hit the men who had brought disaster to his headquarters.

Cody fired into the splintered door three times his direction. The man had had committed suicide. He fell to the floor with two bullets in his heart.

They heard a loud yell from the darkness where the dead man had originated. Another rushed them firing his sidearm and yelling. Bob stopped him with one bullet.

"Those guys are brave!" Cody said. "I hope there's no more."

Bob's left arm had jerked backwards from the first shot. Cody's outside thigh burned slightly from one of the fast rounds. Both of Bob's side arms fell to the floor a second before he did.

Cody stuffed both guns under his belt behind him. He lifted Bob to his feet.

"How bad is it, Bob? I can't see in this darkness!"

"No bone broken but moving is a strain. You?"

"I have a scratch on my right thigh. Let's keep walking. You get behind me. I don't trust you with a rifle."

Bob stiffened. "The bullet severed an artery, Cody. I'm trying to close it off with my right hand."

Cody ripped the sleeve open from the top. "Bob, you're as careless as Leo. I'll tie that off and you can use your off hand to shoot. I just can't believe you let that man get off two shots."

Bob grinned and looked straight ahead. "I think we better find a first aid station fairly quick. Tourniquets are dangerous and you didn't get this one tight enough, I'll bleed out in a few minutes."

Cody quickened his pace and turned where he thought the kitchen might be. He opened another door and found the chef and two helpers sitting quietly by a table.

The cooks jerked back when they spotted the pair. Cody held up his hand and smiled. He spoke in Spanish. "Have no fear. We have no quarrel with you. My friend needs medical attention. Can you help us?"

The chef stood up and one of the assistants left in a hurry. The chef set Bob in his chair and placed his arm on the table gently. His other assistant watched quietly while the chef reached inside his trousers and opened a sharp pocket knife. Cody wondered at some people carrying knives that large and sharp.

The chef worked his blade under the sleeve and cut the shirt sleeve as if it might be paper. More blood flowed quickly. The assistant rushed away and fetched towels and a pot of warm water. They cleaned the wound and the chef pressed his thumb under Bob's left bicep, near the bottom. The other assistant appeared with bandages and ointment.

The chef grinned once and spoke to Bob in English. "My medico supplies are for burns, but the ointment will help the healing. My only worry is keeping the artery closed. The bullet may have damaged muscle tendons in your arm but it missed the bone. Who did this?"

"A man a few doors behind us," Bob said.

"Ahh!" the chef exclaimed. And how is that gentleman?"

"Dead." Bob answered.

"And the Montiagos?" he asked.

"Out of business. Three are alive but retired. "I am sorry to report to you, sir that you and your help here are also out of business."

The chef explained to his assistants what Bob had told him.

One of the assistants sighed and said, "Mi modo!" (My way, meaning such things happen to me.)

Cody said to the chef, "If you search the office of the Montiagos, you might find a money box or a safe. The money you find will hopefully tide you over. If you open the safe, please divide the money among all the people."

The chef grunted an acknowledgement. He translated Cody's words to both assistants. One of them left. The chef asked one to make a pasty out of flour. They would be closing the wound with paste after he held the artery closed for another ten minutes.

The assistant washed his hands thoroughly prior to mixing the paste. The chef called to him and asked him to forget the paste. He nodded to Cody and pointed to the kit for a large bandage.

Cody found it. He opened it and spread a generous amount of ointment to the bandage. The chef took it with one hand and gently laid it over the bullet wound. He said, "We will have to make it tight. Get this man to a hospital as soon as possible. Also, apply ointment to the back of his arm. We will bind his arm and both openings will be sealed."

Cody could think of nothing better to do with the wound. He looked Bob, who appeared slightly faint. "What? Is this the first time you've been wounded? Wake up. We have work waiting for us!"

The chef opened a drawer and pulled two bottles, one bourbon and the other tequila. He offered both to Bob, who refused.

They turned to the door at the sound of running footsteps. The assistant who left carried a sack in one hand and a note in the other. The chef read the note.

"Toda por la gente!" (All for the people!)

The assistant was too excited to stand still. "*Jefe, son ricos! Verdad?*" (*Boss, we are rich. True?*)

The chef nodded negatively. He answered the assistant in Spanish. Cody translated it to Bob.

"No. We have money to feed us until we find employment. This money will be divided among the workers!"

Bob grinned at the chef, who wore a determined face. Although he didn't show it, he felt pleased to have both Bob and Cody's hands on his shoulders for a brief moment. *"Bueno!* We will finish applying the bandage to this man's arm."

His voice remained adamant and tough. Cody knew the man showed them he had a heart but kept his *macho* tone. Cody kept his smile."

The chef asked his assistant in Spanish. "How did you find this?"

The assistant explained. "On a desk! The safe's door was opened!"

The chef nodded. "The Montiagos are good people."

Cody said in Spanish, *"No son arrestados, ellos."* (They are not arrested.)

They bound Bob's arm at the elbow. No blood appeared through the cloth.

They stopped and watched the chef empty the sack of money on the table.

He counted bound stacks of hundred-dollar bills. Many more stacks of bills waited for them in the safe, each worth ten thousand American dollars. He looked up at Bob and Cody. He made an open arm gesture for Cody and Bob to take some of the money. They refused and thanked him. They cautioned the chef to be careful, for if the authorities learned of this, they would take all the money from the people. They also knew that the workers knew this and would live well for a while. Kids would have clothes, as well as the parents, and each family would have a place to live.

They moved further around the building. They passed a room with four guards inside it. They stepped inside but not before the guards had dropped their rifles and stretched their arms toward the ceiling.

Bob kept them covered while Cody removed the large clips from the rifles. He also filled two ten-round clips with five more rounds. They fit well in Bob's pockets.

Cody explained to the men what they would do without question. He ordered them to round up all the workers from the cocaine vats and plantations. They would to assemble in the yard and wait for the chef and assistants. They agreed. One asked if they were under arrest.

Cody nodded negatively. "No. I want you to round up all the workers possible and keep them in the yard. He explained that the Montiagos left money for all of them. The chef will issue the money."

The guards seemed puzzled for a moment then agreed. They, too, would like some money but they usually gained their money from the arrogant lawyer.

Cody explained new orders as they left. "Tell the people in the forest with weapons to drop the weapons and leave them. They could leave or attempt to fight. In such a case, they will receive no money. After they assembled in the yard without weapons, they would be paid.

All four men agreed. Cody doubted if any of them would obey, but four more to the number already out there wouldn't make a difference in a shoot-out.

They found no more people in the large house. They walked back to the girls' room and found Leo talking with the oldest. The men still appeared unconscious. Arrogance still filled the *gringo*. Cody asked him to stand up and walk out the door. He refused to budge.

Cody lifted him to his feet by the shirt's collar and guided him through the doorway.

Once outside, the man dropped to the floor. Cody lifted him by the hair the second time. "Now—*vaquero*—where do you live? What are you doing here?"

"I work in D.C..."

Cody punched his ribs. "You answer me in the exact order I ask. You may not live to brag later."

The man spat out an angry word toward Cody and said, "You know my name. I live in an apartment near Langley, Virginia. I am here to gather information. Who I work for is none of your business."

"How much information have you gathered from these kidnapped teen-agers?"

"I don't partake in that activity. But I do have to know who you people are!"

Cody punched him in his ribs again. He dragged him back inside the girls' room. He asked, let's see the hands of those of you who were molested by this man.

All of them raised their hands, including the youngest, fourteen years of age.

"They're lying!" the *gringo* said. "I've never touched them!"

Bob said, "Don't hit him again, Cody. I think we know who this waste of skin works for. I think we know why he was here. Do you want to tell us to whom the airplane belongs?"

"It belongs to me!"

"Good!" Bob said, "You probably don't mind if we borrow it and return these children home, do you?"

"Yeah, I do mind! If you guys even fly near the Unites States in that plane you'll be blown out of the sky."

"Good!" Leo chimed in. "You will fly us and Cody won't have to do it."

"Of course," the *gringo* agreed, smiling as he said it.

Cody said, "No way! I'm leaving you here, scumbag. You still need to gather more information. How you get back to town or to a telephone is up to you. I'll fly your airplane. Once we're in the states, we'll donate your airplane to a city there. You can write that little number off your inventory."

"Suits me fine." The man responded. "I will have murder charges brought against all of you. That much you can be sure to face once you're in the states."

Leo sat back on the bed and said, "You know something, guys? I don't like this phony excuse for a man. I'm going to erase him."

Cody agreed. "Not a good situation. However, I think we can leave him alive. He's out of work and there's no money to pay him. I'm for allowing him to sort out his self-made situation."

Leo sighed. "We'll only have to return to kill him later."

Cody nodded negatively, "He isn't that much without credentials and his airplane. He's a fed, for certain. I think that he'll be written off their books when he stops delivering money."

Bob said, "Stop it, Cody. His ego is already hurt."

Cody clapped his hands together threw his prisoner on the floor nearest Leo's feet. "I'll take care of the heavy work from here, Bob. Let me have most of your ammo."

Cody removed all the guns from the room and piled the sleeping men in a corner. He then lifted his prisoner to the pile of men and handcuffed him to two separate men. "This will hold you until you manage to escape. If I were you, I'd put escaping off until we are gone. But I think you're smart enough to figure that out for yourself."

He said to Bob, "Watch your arm. That bandage is very tight. We will loosen it if it begins to swell above the bandage."

Cody siphoned two five-gallon cans of gasoline from outside vehicles. He encountered no one from the forest. Back inside he doused gasoline on everything that would burn. When he drew even with the girls' room, he ordered everyone outside. He set that room on fire and tossed a lit match into the kitchen. From there, all of them ran to the nearest house and waited there. He turned all the men loose. The Montiago brothers and son stood by in silence. Everyone knew they had money in banks around the world. Cody took a deep breath and let it out. "Here's where I don't like to be a judge. Any thoughts from you gentlemen?"

"Leave us," the elder Montiago said. "You have my word that you will never hear from us again. That gringo is of no use to anyone here or in your country. Leave him to the forest as you leave us."

"Spoken bravely. You really don't know how true your words are, sir. Your president will put you both in prison if he hears from you. If you rebuild this business, we will return, and that, my man, is what you don't want to happen. If that isn't clear for you, then so be it. Take off. The automobiles are yours, but the gringo and his friends remain here."

By dawn, the big house had burned to the ground. The chef and two assistants were in the other house with the girls. As the pink glow from the sun filtered through the mist of the forest, they saw workers filtering from the woods. Some walked in pairs, others singly.

Cody looked at the chef, who nodded. We are going to give each of them three bills from the U. S. money and five thousand pesos. I think we will have money left over, but I am not sure."

Cody said, "If there is money left over, give it to the kidnapped children from Los Angeles. They are from poor families. I have sent word to the guards in the forest to drop their guns and come back here to be paid. There may be forty or fifty of them."

The chef refused. "I will share nothing with those people. They have been paid more than anyone else."

Cody asked the chef, "Are you certain there's enough money for everyone?"

The chef nodded and pointed to the men walking in their direction. They would be looking for orders without any knowledge of the surprise waiting for them. "We will not see them again. They will settle in Medellin in comfort."

Cody waited until everyone had been paid then set the remaining buildings on fire. He overturned the kerosene drums under the roofs over the vats and set the fuel on fire. The drums exploded and rocketed fifty to one hundred feet into the air.

Back at the people who had assembled, he took the basket of wallets of the men who had been unconscious, including the arrogant *gringo's*. He emptied them into the nearest fire. All Drivers' licenses and paper inside their wallets burned well, including their credit cards. He then advised all the poor workers to leave. They could walk through the forest or go where they pleased. They all left.

After he gave them a half-hour's start, he poured gas over the garage and tossed in a lighted match.

Bob found the man he left in the aircraft and set him free in the woods. He then turned to Cody. "It just occurred to me, Cody, have you ever flown twin turbo props before?"

Cody shook his head negatively. "So this is what a turbo prop looks like. I am impressed. Bob, to be truthful, I don't even know how to crank a jet engine!"

"Well, let's go get the gringo."

Cody lifted a hand. "Now hold on. I said that I didn't know how. I never said that I couldn't."

"Well, how're you going to crank those engines?"

Cody shook his head a bit, feeling a bit overwhelmed. "Bob, just get in the co-pilot's seat after you get these girls loaded. I need to do a little studying in the books and whatever else I can find on the subject."

Leo argued that he would walk. However nervous, he seated himself the in the back after counting the heads of the girls.

After a few moments of reading, Cody started the engines and gave the Check List to Bob. Leo complained but Bob stopped him. In another moment they were airborne. Cody turned the transponder on.

He checked the fuels gages again and concentrated on the nearest route to Las Angeles.

He had to refuel in Hermosillo, Sonora where his credit card might or might not be honored under a careful auditor later in the states.

From there they stopped at the John Wayne International Airport. The authorities detained Cody for not having papers on the aircraft. His NSA papers weighed heavy with everyone, especially the police.

The policeman in charge said, "You've got a little explaining to do, sir. This airplane is registered incognito. Is there any point in asking who you are?"

Cody nodded negatively. "Sorry, sir. Just be aware that I am working on your side. Do you know where my friends are?"

The policeman grinned. "Both got admitted in the hospital for at least an overnight stay. One with a gunshot wound and the other with an ear almost ripped off his head. Can you tell me what the heck happened to you guys in Columbia?"

"Unofficial and off the record with no press?" Cody asked.

"Absolutely! The press is no friend of mine."

Cody nodded positively and grinned at the man's acceptable attitude. "Okay, but pretend that I told you nothing until the three of us are on this plane and out of state."

He returned Cody's nod. "I'm with you."

Cody told him without an explanation of why they were there and that the Colombian Press would be accusing them of murder. The policeman listened with enthusiasm, slapping his fist into the palm of his hand. He said, "Man, I wish I could have been there!"

Cody assured him that he lived in more action in one day on the LAPD than he and his partners lived in a year.

The policeman said, "Well, you're going to have a whole army of press here soon or in the morning that will be making heroes out of you for rescuing those kidnapped high school students. I had even given them up for dead, along with a lot of other people. You really need to be commended for that."

Cody waved it aside. He only gave them a ride. He asked the policeman for help in keeping him and his buddies clear of the press. The man could only say that he would do what he could.

The police notified all the parents of the girls. This lasted almost six hours of steady paperwork and happy reunions before they hospitalized the girls with their parents in tow.

Other parents sat sadly in other benches. Most of the women wept.

Cody's name came up as licensed but not for jets. Once the investigators learned he had flown it from Bogota, they figured that he was thoroughly checked out.

They had waited patiently while the city police located the parents of the kidnapped girls. Once they met their parents, Cody left when the First News people made their noisy appearance. By the time the reporter walked inside the lounge, he had left the building, walking toward a motel.

The doctors released Bob and Leo the following morning. They faced no problem in leaving the John Wayne International Airport. Both men slept in the comfortable seats in the aircraft from an overwhelming amount of painkillers the night before. Cody also expected exhaustion to be consuming them from days of heavy stress. He sighed. In a couple hours he would be their enemy again.

Flying straight for Phoenix, Cody broke north and east looking for a country airstrip somewhere near the city. He found a dirt strip in the pines and planned to land the huge, luxurious airplane on the small strip. As he raced toward the opposite end he shouted at the two men to wake themselves.

"Hey—sleepy heads! Wake up and watch the best landing yet. Ugh—you might want to tighten your safety belts and brace yourselves!"

They did and hardly had time to yell at Cody before he began to exceed the short landing strip. He nosed toward a bush between two large pines. "Cody, no no, man! Don't do this! Please?"

At the same time, Bob yelled, "What's the matter--are you crazy...?"

"Relax, guys! Oh—open the door! Then tighten those seat belts! Relax!

At that time the nose wheel crashed against a pile of dirt piled at the end of the runway. The nose gear collapsed when the right wing caught the first tree. It spun them sharply for a quarter-circle before the other wing caught its destined tree. It stopped abruptly, causing his passengers to grunt and yell again. Both trees caused two sickening bangs as the plane came to its final rest from a high ground speed. Both engines had been obliterated and smoked dangerously amid the hot fumes. Jet fuel did not necessarily need a spark to ignite.

Cody snatched his bag of groceries and headed for the door. Fuel tanks had been ruptured. Leo and Bob stayed on his heels.

"Again?" they both yelled. "Why did you do that? You're sick, Cody! For goodness sake, I cannot believe that you actually did that!"

Cody waited for them to settle down once they cleared the brush and explained. "Guys, this airplane belonged to a federal agency that has a dirty agent smuggling for profit in Colombia. They ain't getting this airplane back. We have seen to that. We're going hide out in the trees again and report in tomorrow at my place in Tucson.

Leo said, "So help me, Cody. I ain't ever flying with you again!"

"Ditto!" Bob said angrily. That's when the fuel on hot metal burst into high flames from spontaneous combustion. The fire reached a fuel tank in less than a second and the concussion from the explosion pinned them down while floating flames above them burned in a cloud of smelly fuel but soon dissipated. A lingering odor swirled around their blistered faces and singed hair.

They made their way into the woods quietly and toward a busy highway of tourists in and out of Phoenix. They ate the groceries Cody had brought and continued to rave on how they hated to fly with him.

Cody didn't bother to explain again. Nothing he could say would stop their unfair and unjust criticisms. He expected the crash to go exactly as it did and he felt proud of his landing skills.

An hour later they caught a ride into Phoenix with a Mormon who claimed he lived near Mormon Lake. Bob enjoyed his company while Cody and Leo slept. Once in Phoenix, Cody called Nancy and she drove to Phoenix to pick them up. All three slept late the next morning in Tucson, except Cody, who woke early with his toddler son pounding his face with a rag toy.

In Tucson and from a pay phone, he called the airport police and explained that the downed airplane used to smuggle narcotics could be found in the trees by a strip north of Phoenix. That's all the information they received. A hundred questions pelted him as he hung up, happy that he could be of assistance.

Two hours later Bob and Leo said their goodbyes, leaving the three men sad in their chests. Leo quickly caught a tear at the corner of his eye while he high-fived Charley. They said nothing more as they caught their commercial flights to cities near their homes.

CHAPTER 32

Cody filled all his time at home playing with his son. His new wife hugged him from behind at each opportunity. After he and his son tired from playing and wrestling on the floor, he finally explained what had taken place. They sat and chatted without Cody mentioning firefights. "No more!" she kept saying.

Cody bounced his son on his knee and kept tossing him into the air. "No more, family. I am retired to take my son fishing and to ball games. You, my dear, can make our living until you sell your business. We're going to be okay financially."

Red called a few hours later and gave him his bank account number and the name of the bank where his passed years' wages had been placed. He also added. "This business of hiring fighters like you guys is expensive, although Congress doesn't mind. Your two buddies are also officially retired. Leo claims that he's going back to Israel with or without my permission."

"I'm sure he can afford it." Cody remarked.

Red chuckled. "The man's bank account is twice as big as yours. So is Bob's."

"I'm concerned over Bob." Cody said. "That woman really did a number on him."

Red said, "I am sorry for that. But...It's been a pleasure, Cody. You are the man they said you were. I think that you'll be interested to know that I'm also retiring. This license to kill business is finished and done. We are the last run of that great idea. Although rumor has it that Immigration is going to get one going."

Cody said, "Okay, boss. Stay clear of it. Don't admit to anything. They will fall on their noses."

"I have one other thing, Cody. The Immigration head doesn't know that I know he's behind this movement but he has asked me if my group had anything to do with those two businesses in Colombia burning down. I told him negative, that my men were all dead."

"Good call," Cody chuckled. "However, I think they had a man at the second ranch we burned. In fact, I'm sure of it. I even took the time to kick that particular tough guy's rear end. They will no doubt depend upon men like him to make them rich. This is why I say they will fall on their noses big time."

Leo spent two days with his parents, gave them enough money to live comfortably for the remainder of their lives and then flew to Israel. He looked up his wife's squadron and joined them. Most of them knew of his fighting skills and felt pleased to have him. Leo, over-joyed to be fighting bad guys again, simply failed to appreciate his good fortune. His first order of business would be to learn their language. At his first chance, he asked about his wife. His superior officer faced him skeptically, shook his head as if amazed, then smiled as he promptly ignored Leo.

Bob settled in his apartment with several bottles of bourbon. His fighting career had finally closed and he felt satisfaction through that. That had to be the emotion of champions, joy and happiness, but only in the sense that he had won many battles. His doctor told him that the chef had done a great job with the bullet wound. Happiness shared between two strangers willing to help one another. Yet he felt no healing. He even grinned at the thought of his arm never having the chance to heal. As one of his final chores at home, he fixed his bank account where it would all go to Lucy in Cagney, West Virginia. This would happen after some hapless passerby discovered his stinking corpse.

He stared blankly at the telephone, seriously considering yanking it from its wires before starting on the bottles. He knew the time had finally arrived to fall asleep permanently.

Sitting on the edge of his bed where he planned to be for the remainder of his life, he muttered to himself, "Okay, Bob, I'll try one more time but only because you're insisting. Another refusal cannot hurt me worse."

The telephone in the Moore's residence in Cagney rang. The same gruff voice answered.

Bob sighed but he would deal with the man one more time. "It's me, Dennis. Can I please speak with...?"

Lucy snatched the telephone from her dad.

"Dennis—Dennis! Is that you?"

"None other," he replied with sadness still controlling his voice.

She talked rapidly. "Dennis, I have had time to think. Can you ever forgive me? I am so sorry! Please forgive me! I'm begging!"

At first, Bob refused to believe what he heard. *She's probably tired of living with her dad.* Nevertheless, he felt his heart began to beat joyously again. He would have her under any circumstance. In one of his many feelings he thought that he could actually feel life flowing through his veins. The pressing air weighing heavily on his shoulders began to lighten.

"Oh—I think so. We do have a bit of catching up to do."

She was almost too excited to answer. "I'm here, my darling! I'll be here!"

The End

EPILOGUE

This concludes the epic Cody Hunter series of four.

Due to his exceptional talent with firearms and his ability to move fast, Cody was drafted into an elite, highly secretive organization of only a few men with the same talent.

Cody paired with two men that could move and shoot like comic book heroes. They explained the ropes to him on the job while he endured their own brand of humor and harmless initiation processes that never ceased.

The three of them first played havoc with two highly successful cartels headquartered between Bogota and Medellin. Next they flew to Iraq to crush Saddam Husseins's prodigious accumulation of nuclear weapons. As soon as they concluded their stay in Iraq, they unknowingly, assisted President Reagan's Star Wars Project in Hawaii.

After almost three years, the cartels hired a small band of expensive mercenaries to seek out and destroy the trio in the United States. This was their error.